TRAILS TO
P·O·O·S·E·Y

Written by **OLIVE R. COOK**
Author of *Serelda's Star* and *Locket*

♦

Illustrated by **CHELSEA SAMMEL**

D0104543

Misty Hill Press
Sebastopol, California

Book Design, Cover Design: Hildegard Pressesky
Illustrations: Chelsea K. Sammel
Typography: Publications Services of Marin

Library of Congress Cataloging-in-Publication Data

Cook, Olive Rambo, 1982–1981
Trails to Poosey.

Summary: Young Nathan, growing up as part of a
homesteading family in Missouri in 1830, faces danger
in the wilderness when he must go in search of his
missing father.
[1. Frontier and pioneer life—Missouri—Fiction.
2. Missouri—Fiction]   I. Title.
PZ7.C772Tr   1986   [Fic]   86-8602
ISBN 0-930079-01-9

Thanks to George Cook for meticulously reviewing and proofreading his mother's last manuscript.

♦

Thanks to Charles Cornue for his ongoing support of the project and assistance in obtaining resource material about Missouri in the 1830's.

♦

We especially thank the State Historical Society of Missouri whose personnel searched exhaustively through files for photographs and supporting material to aid in making the book's illustrations authentic to the time and place of the story.

♦

The publisher also extends thanks, for the author, to the many persons and organizations who furnished help and information to Olive Cook during her preparation and writing of the manuscript.

Misty Hill Press
Sebastopol, California

FOREWORD

In the 1830's pioneers came from Kentucky, Virginia and Tennessee to settle northern Missouri. One family came from Garrard County, Kentucky, across the creek from Poosey Ridge, to a place in the northwest corner of what is now Livingston County, Missouri, between the forks of Grand River. The new country with its steep hills and little hollows reminded them so much of their native land that they called it Poosey, after Poosey Ridge, Kentucky, and the name has hung on to this day.

Poosey has never been on a map, or had a set boundary, yet oldtimers and even present day folk will tell you, "It's down the road a piece," "Over the ridge yonder," or "You jes' came through it."

The Robisons are an imaginary family, in a historic setting. Some of the names in my story are of real people and places—Jesse Nave, who founded the trading post of Navestown, which grew into a village later called Springhill; Captain William Jack, who established a ferry across the Missouri River at Lexington; and also Reverend Finus Ewing at the Land Office. These were real people, but given new personalities by the author.

Today the steep hills and little hollows of Poosey have not changed much. The entrance to Panther Cave has been closed, but if you scrape away the moss from the rock cliff underneath the cave, you can still find the carved names of pioneers, some of them dating back to the early

OLIVE RAMBO COOK

1800's. You might, if you looked closely enough, see the names of Pa and Nathan and Betsy and Dick and Walkfast, who surely must have gone that way. There might even be the tiny carved hoofprint of a colt named Trinket.

Olive R. Cook
Mountain View, California

—≫ CHAPTER 1 ≪—

It was the middle of July, 1837, and a hot, still day. Nathan Robison, astride his tired mare, Kentucky Belle, brought up the rear of the pack train.

Ahead on the narrow trail he caught glimpses through the trees of his father leading the way on Major, the big bay, a glint of sunshine on his rifle. Single file behind Pa came Ma on Charlie. After Ma came his sister Betsy on Spot with four-year-old Andy hugged against her. Following Betsy were the two pack mules loaded with the belongings of the family, including the precious Seth Thomas clock, seed for starting a garden and two cuttings from the lilac bush by Grandma's front door.

Nathan had tied on his saddle the bundle of books wrapped in oilcloth with Pa's fiddle case fastened on the top.

This had been the order all the long miles from Kentucky to the forks of Grand River in north Missouri. Pa had led the way, and Nathan had brought up the rear with Shep, the dog, running back and forth often so tired and footsore that Nathan lifted him up on the saddle to let him ride.

A few days before, Belle had hurt her leg and now she stumbled. Nathan slipped his rifle underneath the straps that held it upright and slid to the ground to walk along beside her.

"We're about there old girl," he told her. "This is the last day; then you'll have two whole weeks to rest before your foal comes." The mare nickered softly.

"Why," Nathan pondered as he trudged along, "did Pa want to come to Missouri? Why couldn't he have let us stay in our good log cabin in Kentucky near Grandma and Grandpa? Then I could have gone with Grandpa when he called on patients and learned how to be a doctor. Grandpa said I had a natural bent for it, but Pa didn't think so. Pa thinks you owe it to your folks to stay with them to help until you are of age, like the law says.

"The minute I'm twenty one, I'll go back to Kentucky, though, to study to be a doctor, even if I can't get a license to practice until I'm an old gray-headed man!"

A shout up front brought Nathan alert. Betsy turned in her saddle and waved her hand. "Nathan! I see a cabin! We're here! We're here!"

Nathan looked up. He could see a roof! Two roofs! He hurried his steps forgetting he was tired and homesick.

The green light that sifted down through the tall tree-tops changed to bright sunlight as they came into the

clearing. There were several log cabins along a dusty road. A sign over a double one read—NAVESTOWN TRADING POST.

Two dogs ran out barking furiously, Shep growled and walked stiff-legged toward the strangers. Nathan led Belle up beside his mother. "Ma, we're finally here," he said his voice rough with excitement. "Are you plumb tired out?"

Ma pushed back her sunbonnet and smiled at him. "No, but I'm surely thankful to be here."

A stocky boy about Nathan's age came out yelling at the dogs and a big, square-shouldered man followed. Pa dismounted and walked over to the man.

"Are you Jesse Nave?" Pa asked.

"Yes, I am. Are you folks travelin' or goin' some place?"

Pa chuckled. "Neither one right now. I'm Peter Robison. We're from Poosey Ridge, Garrard County, Kentucky, nigh Lancaster. Left there the last of April. Heard there was some real fine land up this way, with lots of game and plenty of water." Pa turned and looked at Ma. "That's my wife Marthy, Betsy my daughter goin' on twelve and Andy the least one. Nathan here is the eldest. Turned fifteen since we started."

Jesse Nave nodded his head and spoke to Ma, then turned to the boy beside him. "This is my son, Dick. Turn him loose in the woods and he can track like an Indian."

Dick's face flushed. He looked at Nathan and their eyes met. For a moment they measured each other, then Dick grinned and Nathan smiled back.

"Come in and rest yourselves and meet the Missus. You look kinda tuckered out, Mrs. Robison," Jesse Nave said as he held up his hand to help her down. "We'll be glad to share what we have, poor as it is."

Ma got down from the horse and smoothed her dress. "I had a little sick spell after we started," she said. "I just haven't felt real pert since then, but as soon as we're settled I'll be all right."

A stout, blond woman came down the path carrying a baby on her hip, one little girl holding on to her skirt and an older girl walking behind her. Jesse Nave called out, "Isabella, this is the Robisons, came clear from Kentucky a-horseback. Been travelin' since last of April."

Isabella looked at them, a friendly smile on her round face. She nodded a greeting to each one. "Sakes, you've come a far piece. I know, for we're from Tennessee, but we came in a wagon. Come in and make yourselves to home. We aim to have supper pretty soon. Nothin' extra, but you're welcome. My, it's been hot today, ain't it?"

"You can unsaddle and leave the plunder here under the tree," Jesse said. "Dick, you go with Nathan to water the horses."

With the Naves helping, the horses and mules were soon unsaddled. Pa took the grub box and the fiddle with him as he went with Jesse to the cabin.

Dick picked up a box. "Must be rocks in this," he grunted.

"It's books," Nathan said as he carried the clock box.

"Books?" Dick was astonished. "This many books?"

"Yes, mostly school books except for the Bible. Ma's strong on learning. She went to Normal school in Virginia and was going to be a teacher, but she married Pa. Her father, Grandpa Scott, is a doctor. He's strong on learning, too. Now, Pa, he's not so strong, but he can sing and play the fiddle."

Dick looked at Nathan. "I can say the letters and write my name and do the tables to the sixes," he said proudly. "Pa taught me. I want to be a boat captain when I grow up and Pa says they have to know a lot."

"A boat captain on the Grand River?"

"No, on the Big Missouri, or maybe even the Mississippi. Pa's got a flat boat he takes to Brunswick and I went with him once and I liked it." For a moment they were quiet, then Dick turned to Nathan. "What are you going to be?"

"A doctor," Nathan said firmly.

Dick caught his breath. "A doctor?"

Nathan nodded as he took off Belle's saddle and put it over the package of books and the clock box. "I rode around with Grandpa sometimes. Once I helped him sew up a bad cut in a man's leg and another time I helped to set a boy's broken arm."

"Then why did you come here? Why didn't you stay with your Grandpa?"

"Because Pa needed me to ride trail and help build the new cabin. He says wanting to be a doctor is just a fool idea I got from Grandpa; that I'll soon get over wanting to be one. But I won't!"

Dick looked sympathetically at Nathan. "Grown folks don't always know, do they?"

"No they don't."

Nathan and Dick led the horses and the mules followed. The spring came out of a rock ledge and ran into a hollowed-out log resting on two big rocks. The horses and mules crowded around drinking deeply. A gourd dipper hung on a tree branch and Nathan filled it under the stream and had a drink. "My, that's good and cold. I hope Pa finds a place with a spring like that."

"It won't be hard. Nobody much lives over that-a-way, 'cept some Injuns in the summer and wild animals." Dick swept his arm in a wide circle toward the northwest. "It's just steep hills and little hollers covered with rocks and big trees. Lots of springs."

"Indians?"

Dick nodded. "But they're not mean. Pa gets along with Injuns fine and he won't let anyone around here fight 'em when they come to trade their furs and wampum. There's an old buryin' place way up on the high hill. Walkfast showed me. We're friends. The tribe goes south in the winter and comes back in the summer going north.

"We saw some Indians after we left Brunswick village and there was an Indian camp at the mouth of a big creek, but it looked deserted."

The boys hobbled the horses and mules then turned them loose, all except Belle. She was picketed with a long rope. "She's my own mare," Nathan said as he tied the knot. "Grandpa gave her to me when I was eleven. She's to have her colt in two weeks. She slipped and fell two days ago and she hadn't been doing very well even before that. It might make the colt come sooner."

"Might," Dick agreed.

As they walked toward the cabin, Dick looked at Nathan and smiled, his blue eyes warm and friendly. "Seems like you ain't no stranger," he said shyly.

"I feel that way, too," Nathan said earnestly, a new warmth in his heart.

Dick pointed to the cabin nearest the Naves. Two girls were standing in the door, one about the age of Betsy. "Chaffins live there. They came in 1832, the year after we did. They have four girls, no boys." He shrugged.

He pointed to the left of the clearing. "Slatons live there, a girl and two boys littler than me. The Ma and Pa both been ailin' with chills and fever.

"Over there's the Radabaughs and next to them the Lamsons. Sam Radabaugh can make real good boots or mend your old ones.

"The Lamsons had hard luck. Little girl died last winter then the baby about a month ago. Mrs. Lamson cries a lot and begs him to go back to Ohio where their folks are. But he doesn't want to go.

"Think maybe your Pa will want to build here in the settlement?" Dick asked as they walked toward the cabins.

"Don't think so," Nathan said thoughtfully. "That's why he left Kentucky. Said it was getting too crowded. Pa's restless and wants to keep moving. Always looking for a better place. My sis is just like him. But Ma and me are different, we want to take root," Nathan said gravely. "We didn't want to leave Kentucky."

"There ain't no better place than this," Dick said firmly. "Your Pa will stay here."

But Nathan wondered.

—≫ CHAPTER 2 ≪—

ick and Nathan walked to the trading post and went inside. It was a big room with shelves and a counter at each end and a fireplace in the center of the side wall. Pa was looking at a two-man crosscut saw. "Think you could manage one end of this?" he asked Nathan.

"Guess I could try," Nathan answered, thinking of all the logs it would take to build the cabin, first to cut the trees, then to trim and notch them. He hadn't been old enough to help when his father built the one in Kentucky.

Jesse Nave stood behind the counter at the west end of the room and "store things" were on the shelves behind him and on the end of the counter. There were split-hickory baskets, wooden and tin buckets, a bolt of turkey red calico, another bolt of black with white flowers. Saws, axes, hammers, froes, rives and whetstones and scythes. A lantern with a place for a candle, crocks of different sizes and a stone churn with a wooden dasher, and other articles. At one side stood a barrel of salt and one of cornmeal.

"Pa will barter for anything in the store except the salt. Folks have to pay cash for that," Dick said matter-of-factly.

There was a rank smell and Nathan traced it to the other end of the room where piles of cured hides lay on the floor or hung in bundles from the ceiling. That half of the room seemed almost full of hides and furs and beeswax in wooden barrels.

"Pa hangs the skunk pelts outside so that it won't smell so bad in here." Dick grinned as Nathan wrinkled his nose.

"Do you pack the goods in overland from Brunswick?"

"No, most of it by flatboat," Jesse Nave answered. "I built my own boat to float down on when the river's up. I'm getting ready now to take down a load of hides and furs. I bring back provisions for the store. Take a man along to help pole us back. I'm getting a late start this time. Aim to go on to St. Louis where I hope prices will be better."

"We crossed the ferry at St. Louis. Spent a day and two nights. Regular boom town and everything sky high. Thousands of people there and lots of going and coming on the river."

By suppertime Nathan almost felt at home. The Naves called the floored, roofed-over space between the cabin and the store the "dog-trot", just like folks did in Kentucky. Here he helped Dick make a long table with a couple of sawhorses and boards laid across. The girls helped by putting around the plates, knives and forks. It would be good to sit down at a table to eat your bread and meat out here in the cool of the day.

Ma offered to help but Isabella said, "I'm not doing much, just making an extra pan of corn pone and putting more onions in the stew. But it would help a heap if you'd mind the baby. He's teethin' and been fretting all day."

After awhile they all sat down on benches around the table. Jesse Nave asked Pa to say the blessing. Pa thanked the Lord for a safe trip from Kentucky to Missouri and for finding such fine neighbors.

Nathan was almost ashamed he ate so much. Big bowls of well-seasoned stew were passed around and heaping plates of cornpone followed with comb honey and butter for spreading. And to top it off, a big glass of milk cooled in the spring house.

"Best meal since we left Kentucky," Pa said as they finished.

"Cost you plenty," Jesse Nave said firmly as they got up from the table.

Nathan stared. Folks never charged when strangers came by in Kentucky.

Pa stopped stone-still and squared his shoulders. "Don't have a lot of money," he said, "but I'm willing to work. Name your price."

Jesse Nave's blue eyes twinkled. "Just limber up your fiddle and give us some tunes. I get as hungry for music as I do for vittles."

Pa chuckled and Nathan felt relieved. "Nothin' I'd

rather do than oblige you," he said and took the violin from the case.

Mrs. Nave invited Ma to sleep in the house on one of the children's beds and Ma accepted. Nathan and Betsy made pallets for Pa and Andy and themselves out in the yard by the big tree. Then Dick and Nathan carried out stools and benches to put in front of the cabin where the grown folks could sit and listen. The children could sit on the ground.

Pa sat on a stool in front and got what Betsy called his "fiddlin' look", tuned the instrument and began to play. Pa was a handsome man with a shock of curly dark hair and soft dark eyes. Sometimes his clear tenor voice was so wistful and haunting it made little shivers run up Nathan's spine and he felt sad and lonely; but other times when Pa fiddled a fast one, Nathan wanted to laugh and run and shout.

Pa began with a gay tune and his voice filled the soft summer evening. He hadn't finished the song before the other folk in the village began coming and sat down quietly on the grass.

When there was a stopping place, Mr. Nave said, "Folks this is Peter Robison and Marthy his wife from Poosey Ridge, Kentucky,—their three children, Nathan, Betsy and Andy. They are going to be our neighbors." Somebody clapped and Nathan felt his face flush in the darkness.

Soon folks joined in the singing of familiar songs. Nathan lay back on the grass. Tomorrow Dick was going to take him and his father back in the hills to hunt for a homesite. Ma and Betsy would do some washing while they were close to water and could use a bench and Mrs. Nave's washpot. He sure hoped Pa would pick out a site close to the settlement with a spring near at hand.

A horse squealed and another whinnied. Nathan slipped away from the group, Shep at his heels, and hurried to Belle, but Belle seemed all right. She nuzzled Nathan's arm. "Tomorrow," he told her, "Pa is going to look for a spot to settle, so hold off borning your colt if you can." He leaned against her and stroked her side.

He got the bottle of liniment from a bundle and rubbed some on the mare's sore leg. It didn't seem quite so swollen and tender now. As he replaced the bottle he decided he would go to bed. With walking most of the day to save the strain on Belle's leg, he was bone-tired and already half-asleep. He took off his boots and lay down.

He thought of Dick. It seemed he had known him a long time. It would be good to have a friend, but if Pa picked out a place far away he might not see him often. He looked up into the starry sky and singled out the Big Dipper and the North Star. It was comforting to know they never changed, they would be there forever. He wondered if Grandpa was out on a call and might be looking at them, too. "Will I ever get to be a doctor?" he mumbled to himself as he drifted off into a troubled sleep, the fiddle music weaving through his dreams.

—⟫ CHAPTER 3 ⟪—

In the morning they ate breakfast with the Naves, hot corn cakes with butter and honey and crisp side meat and cups of sassafras tea. Ma kept talking about the tasty tea, but Nathan could hardly swallow it.

"Dick will take you up north and west where it's not settled. He knows it even better than I do, tramped all over it with Walkfast. Lots of big timber and springs. But you better change your mind and settle here in Navestown," Naves advised.

Nathan caught the look on his mother's face and knew she would like to live in the settlement where she could have close neighbors.

Pa shook his head. "Too crowded," he said.

They were soon ready. Nathan rode Sam, one of the pack mules, so that Belle could rest. Pa rode Major and Dick one of the Nave's horses. It was just like yesterday only Dick took the lead with Nathan in the middle and Pa following.

They angled to the northwest. The air was sweet with the scent of honey locust blossoms that hung from the trees in creamy-white clusters. Pa said he had never seen such white oaks and hickories.

The hills got steeper with narrow valleys. In many places they had to walk to keep from being pushed off the horses' backs by low growing tree limbs and dense thickets. Shadows were dark with over-lapping tree tops making a green twilight through which they struggled, stopping often to rest.

Finally at the top of a high steep hill, they came out on an open place with sandstone ledges cropping out.

"Watch out for rattlesnakes," Dick cautioned. "They have dens underneath and come out on the rocks to sun themselves." They dismounted, walked to the edge of the cliff and looked almost straight down for nearly a hundred and fifty feet. A creek shone silver at the bottom.

They were on the west side of a valley. Pa stood looking and motioning, measuring with his hand. "About a quarter of a mile long and maybe thirty rods wide," he guessed as they looked down on the treetops. Across the valley they could see for miles until the green hills turned to misty blue and faded into the skyline.

"Highest place around," Dick said, "but for one over southeast where the Indians have a burying ground. We call it Indian Hill."

Nathan looked far away into the distance. It was the

top of the world and they were standing on the rim looking over.

"Let's go," Pa said. "Nice place to look out, rests your soul, but no water up here and too rocky for crops."

As they started away a chilling scream like a hurt woman came from somewhere to the north of the valley. The horses threw up their heads. Nathan caught his breath.

"Panther," Pa said softly. "Don't usually scream like that in the daytime."

"Sounds like it was down toward Panther Cave," Dick said.

"You mean panthers live in a cave?" Nathan asked in disbelief.

"No, but some trappers killed a panther in the cave and its been called that ever since. Pa and I saw a panther last winter, coming right down the trail at us, wind behind him. Yellowish like, with a white belly. About five feet long, not counting its tail. Pa said it would have weighed ninety or a hundred pounds. Just for a second it stared straight at us, then it leaped and was gone. Pa was so shocked he never aimed his gun. Made my hair stand on end." Dick shivered, remembering.

Nathan did not say anything. Killing things just to be killing made him sick. He was grateful that Pa never killed except for food. Seemed even panthers and bears had a right to live unless they threatened you. Grandpa said all life was precious.

They found their way around the steep sides of the hill

and came down into the far end of the valley they had seen from the cliff. It was more open than it had looked from above. The land was gently rolling, mostly covered with timber. Some of the white oak trees were over three feet through and so high it made Nathan dizzy when he looked at the tops. There were some places where bluestem grass was belly deep on the horses.

They rode the length of the valley and came back to the foot of the high cliff they had stood on up above. A spring flowed out of the cliff and fed the creek. Pa said this was a good place to rest and eat their dinner.

Horses and men drank their fill. The water was cool and sweet. They rested in the shade of a huge cottonwood tree and ate the victuals Mrs. Nave had tied up in a cloth.

Nathan liked the valley. He wished Pa would decide on this very place. He felt happier than he had since leaving Kentucky. Suddenly he knew why. "Pa," he said quickly. "This place makes me think of home in Poosey Ridge. The hills, the creek, the little hollers, everything! With Lancaster about where Navestown is! Doesn't it seem that way to you?"

Pa looked surprised, then glanced around them. "You're right. It does seem like the country around Poosey. I feel right comfortable, like I'd been here before and that's why. It's like Poosey Ridge!"

"How far is it to Navestown?" Nathan asked.

Dick looked at the sun and calculated for a moment. "Maybe three miles straight across. Can't rightly say we wound around so much."

"About five I judge, the way we came," Pa said.

Nathan was glad. Five miles from Navestown was no distance at all, even though the hills were high. Still, Pa might think it too close. Pa wanted to live away from people, yet other times he wanted to be right in the middle of a crowd playing his fiddle and singing to beat everything. It was almost like having two fathers.

Pa dug into the soil with his hands. It was loose and loamy. "Leaves rotted here since time began." He crumbled the soil and let it fall through his fingers. "New land! Never felt a plow. Grow anything!" He got up from his knees and dusted off his hands on his breeches. He looked back the way they had come, then over at the creek with the flowing spring. A smile spread over his face. He turned to Dick with a look in his dark eyes Nathan had never seen before. "No need to look farther. If this land ain't entered we'll settle right here. Best place I've ever seen." Pa turned to Nathan. "What do you think?"

"Oh Pa," Nathan was surprised at Pa asking, "I like it with the spring so close and the hills and hollers like Poosey. And it's not far from Navestown. I think Ma and Betsy would like it, too."

"I don't think it has been entered," Dick said, "but wouldn't it be awful hard gettin' to it, comin' the way we did?"

"I'll take a sighting and we'll go back a different way," Pa answered. "Keep to the level as much as we can."

They started back, this time with Pa leading. He followed the creek, whenever possible as it went around the hills. Nathan felt sure the trail was longer, but not so hard to travel. They might find a shortcut later. Several times they saw deer and once three startled antelope flashed before them. Under a huge oak tree they saw where a flock of wild turkeys roosted.

Dick yelled at Pa to turn to the right and he would hit the trail that led into Navestown. They were soon there.

"We found the perfect spot!" Pa called out jubilantly as Ma and Betsy came from the cabin. "Fine little holler with a creek and a spring right by. Marthy, you can pick out the very spot you want the cabin built. Nathan has already named it Poosey!"

"Poosey!" Ma said the name and smiled at Nathan.

"How far is it from here?" Betsy asked.

"I judge about four miles the long way," Pa said, "but not more than three the way the crow flies."

"That's not so far," Betsy said.

"Did you see a bear?" Andy asked solemnly.

Pa smiled and ruffled Andy's blond hair. "No, but we heard a panther scream."

"Panthers!" Ma frowned.

"It was a long way off," Dick said.

"Will it be far to carry water?" Betsy asked again.

"No, it's right handy. The spring comes out of a ledge on the side of the cliff, and the creek makes a little turn. Finest spot to live I've ever seen."

Dick described the location. "Is it spoke for?" he asked his father.

Jesse Nave thought about it. "No, it's all government

land. Surveyed, but don't know if recorded. Welcome to all you can pay for at $1.25 an acre, but you have to go to Lexington with your gold to enter at the land office. That's quite a piece from here. Must be close to seventy-five or eighty miles and only bee trails to follow. Then months later you have to go back again and get the patent papers. I made two trips and sure glad it's over."

Nathan and Dick unsaddled the horses and Sam, watered and hobbled them then turned them loose. Nathan went to Belle. She heard him coming and whinnied a greeting and rubbed her nose against his sleeve.

He felt her sides, frowning as he did so. Then he looked at her udder and it was filling. He squatted down looking closely at her leg. "It's better, but I'll wait until bedtime to put on more liniment," he told her. He stood up and looked into her brown eyes. "Pa found a place and we'll go out tomorrow, so you hold off having that colt until we get there. You mind me. It never could walk that far." He petted her again, and she nickered softly as he turned away. All the signs said that the colt was coming too soon.

They ate supper again with the Naves and had more stew and corn pone, but there was no singing or fiddling afterward. Instead Pa dickered with Mr. Nave for the saw, a wedge, an axe for Nathan and a hoe for Betsy, a tin bucket and iron kettle for Ma and cornmeal for everyone. Nathan was real proud when Pa handed over a gold piece to pay for them.

Once more Ma slept in the cabin and the rest of the family under the trees.

—≫ CHAPTER 4 ≪—

I t was coming daylight when Nathan was startled awake. Shep was whining and licking his face. Half-asleep, he pushed the dog away pulling the quilt around his shoulders. Then a soft sound alerted him. He raised up on his elbow and listened. He jerked on his boots and hurried toward the place where Belle was staked out. He knew before he got there that the foal had come. It lay on the grass and Belle was making soft loving sounds, licking and nudging it, trying to get it to stand.

Nathan knelt and looked at it. It was a tiny mare foal, a reddish bay like Belle. He stroked its little nose and patted the damp curly mane and forelock. "You came a little early," he said softly, "but we're glad to have you."

It was so small and thin Nathan wondered if it had any strength at all. It was almost dry and should have stood up and nursed by this time, but Belle's udder was full. Once it struggled to stand and fell back exhausted.

"Never you mind," Nathan said soothingly, "I'll help you get your breakfast." He lifted the foal in his arms and pushed its nose against it's mother's udder, but it would not even try to nurse.

For a minute Nathan held the foal, urging it to suck, then he laid it back on the ground and ran to where Betsy was just waking. "Come quick! I need help! Belle's had her foal and it can't suck."

Pa wakened and raised up. "What's the matter? What's wrong?"

"The foal's come," Nathan said over his shoulder.

Betsy came stumbling behind him, groggy with sleep. Nathan lifted the foal again and held its lips against Belle's udder. "Now, push a teat in its mouth," he told Betsy, "and hold it there. Maybe it will suck."

Belle was excited and nervous and would not stand still.

"Whoa Belle! Stand still! We're trying to help!" Nathan scolded.

Finally Betsy got the teat in the foal's mouth and kept it there. Nathan's arms and back were aching with the weight of the foal when Pa came up behind them.

"There! It's sucking! It swallowed!" Betsy cried out. "Whoa Belle! Nathan make Belle stand still. It took another swallow."

"Here," Pa said behind them, "let me hold awhile. Maybe it can stand now. Put it down and let's see."

Nathan held the little foal up, but when he loosened

his hold it crumpled to the ground. Pa knelt down and felt its legs and moved them. "It's got limberleg," he said sadly and straightened up.

"What's limberleg?" Nathan's voice shook.

"The bones don't stiffen as they should and are limber. Sometimes even babies have it and their legs bow out, but babies can nurse until the bones harden. Animals with limberleg can't stand up to nurse."

"You mean it will die because it can't stand to suck?" Nathan choked over the words.

"It would probably die anyway," Pa said. "I never saw such a puny, weak little colt. Maybe the trip was too hard on Belle, with no grain. But she can have another colt sometime," Pa comforted. "Best just to put it out of its misery. You and Betsy go on up to the house and I'll do it for you."

"No! No! Pa it's got to live! I'll find some way to make it live!"

"You can't make bones," Pa said. "Just let me get rid of it now before everyone wakes up."

"No, Pa! Not now! It's not had a chance. Give me time, I'll think of something," Nathan pleaded.

"Just wanting the foal to live won't save it!" Pa said sharply and walked away.

Betsy wiped the tears from her eyes. "Hold it up again Nathan, it was beginning to suck. When I get awful hungry my legs get weak. Maybe that's all that's wrong."

Nathan picked up the foal again talking softly to Belle. Betsy guided the teat into the foal's mouth and soon little suds of milk leaked from its lips. At last it had its fill and was tired out. It trembled and its head fell to one side as Nathan laid it down. Belle began to lick her eyes closed and she went to sleep.

Betsy and Nathan were quiet as they watched the tiny foal.

"I helped Grandpa put splints on that man's leg when he broke it. I don't see why splints on the colt's legs wouldn't work the same way. Not put splints over the joints, just between the joints, then her legs would move and she could get up and down to eat while her legs grew stronger."

"Oh Nathan, I knew you'd think of something! Let's try it. I'll help you do anything to save her. She's such a cute little tyke, no bigger than a trinket. Let's name her, too."

Nathan smiled for the first time. "I think you just named her. We'll call her Trinket." He looked down at the foal so frail and tiny. "You're Trinket," he said and patted it lovingly. Then he stood up and stroked Belle's neck. "We're going to try everything to make your foal live."

They walked back to the cabin, the sun making long shadows across the clearing. Breakfast was ready and Ma looked rested. "Too bad about the colt, Nathan," she said putting her hand on his arm. "But Belle can have another one."

"There's just nothing you can do for limberleg," Jesse Nave said. "Shame, too, for your Pa says the mare's a thoroughbred and the colt full-blooded, too."

"But Nathan has thought of something to try," Betsy spoke up, "and I think it will work."

Nathan saw the doubt in their eyes as the men looked at him. "Once I helped Grandpa put splints on a man's broken leg so I'm going to put splints on the colt's legs, not over the joints, just between. Then maybe she can stand up to suck until they get strong."

Pa frowned, unconvinced. "If you want to try you can," he said to Nathan, "but we're going to pack up and start to the land right after breakfast. You can carry the colt on Belle, but you'll have to do the splinting over there."

Dick looked at Nathan, his blue eyes shining; then he turned to his father, "Can I go along to help?"

Jesse Nave smiled at his son. "Yes, you can take some of the things on your horse, since there's the extra load of the colt."

—≫| CHAPTER 5 |≪—

ithin an hour they were ready to go, Pa leading on
Major, Ma next, then Betsy and Andy on Spot followed by the two pack mules, Sam and Bill. Dick came
after with the new tools, bucket and cornmeal on one side
and the box of books on the other. This time, Ma was carrying the fiddle. Pa carried the new iron kettle with some
coals in ashes from the Nave's fireplace.

Nathan came last on Belle, the little colt in his arms,
resting across the saddle in front of him.

All the neighbors came out to see them leave.

"We sure are much obliged for all the vittles and
visitin' and such," Pa said when they were ready to go.
"Feels like home already. Now you come and see us. When
we get a door, it will be open to you!"

Ma thanked them, too.

"You still owe me," Jesse Nave told Pa. "Didn't get to hear near all the tunes I wanted. Come back soon and we'll get the folks together and have a singing bee."

"We'll sure do that," Pa answered waving. "Goodby."

"Remember what I told you!" Jesse Nave called. "When you get ready to heist the logs let me know. I'll send out the word and we'll have a 'log rollin', remember?"

"I'll remember," Pa called back.

They stopped often. Pa cut off small, low-hanging tree limbs, or lopped off bushes sticking out across the trail. Once Dick helped Nathan hold the foal and she drank hungrily without urging. Then she slept the rest of the way. Belle worried and made soft anxious sounds and turned her head often to look at the foal. "She's all right. She's fine," Nathan assured the mare, but he was anxious too, wondering if the frail little foal would live. Would she have the strength to walk after the splints were on? He would read in the doctor book that Grandpa gave him the minute he had time. Grandpa always said, "What's good for humans is good for animals."

The sun was straight overhead when they reached the valley. Pa stopped and dismounted then helped Ma down. "Marthy, this is our holler. Ain't it plumb beautiful? Doesn't it make you think of Poosey?"

Ma took off her sunbonnet and looked all around at the flowing creek, the little waterfall, the high bluff above, the towering trees with scattering patches of tall bluestem grass between. Her face lighted up, she looked at Pa and smiled. "It does look like Poosey, for a fact."

Dick held the foal while Nathan tied Belle to a tree, then they laid the foal on the grass beside her.

"I'm empty to my boot tops," Pa said. "Let's eat a piece, then we'll unload and pick out the homesite."

It was more cornpone and fried side meat, but with cold water from the spring, it tasted good. The animals were unloaded and hobbled. They made camp by the creek where the family would live until the shed was finished.

Nathan and Dick found some flat stones to make a hollow square for the fire. They drove two forked sticks into the ground with a trimmed sapling laid across to swing the kettle on. Nathan built the fire with the coals from Nave's fireplace and filled the kettle from the creek. "Handiest place we've ever camped," Nathan said gratefully, as he hung the kettle over the fire.

Pa and Betsy tied a rope between two trees and hung the tarpaulin over it, pulled out the corners and staked them down. It had been a nightly chore ever since they left Kentucky.

Once more Dick and Nathan held the foal up to nurse. She began eagerly, switching her fuzzy tail as she drank. Soon drops of milk were leaking out of her mouth. When she had finished, Nathan stroked her head.

"Let's hurry and get the splints on its legs," Dick said. "I want to see if it can stand up. What will you do if it can't?"

Nathan looked at Dick, his dark eyes troubled. "I'll just keep on holding her up 'til she's so big I can't lift her. What I'll do then, I won't think about."

While Ma and Pa went to choose the homesite, the

children looked for saplings. "Bark from slippery elm or hickory will come off easy," Dick said.

Not far from camp, they found some hickory saplings; Nathan cut two and they dragged them back to camp. There, they measured the length between the joints of Trinket's front legs. They split the bark lengthwise then peeled it off. Very carefully, Nathan placed the bark around the colt's front leg above the knee. It overlapped about an inch. "Cut me a long thin shaving, Dick, and I'll use it to tie with." The shaving worked fine with Nathan wrapping it around and holding it while Betsy tied it in a hard knot and tucked the ends under.

"We'll do the front legs, for it gets up on those first. Maybe we won't have to tie the hind ones."

Belle had been quiet with the foal beside her, but after they moved it away from her and began working on it, she grew uneasy and strained on the halter rope trying to reach it.

Dick held the foal's other leg and Nathan placed the bark around it above the knee and Betsy wrapped the shaving around and tied it. Then they "barked" the legs below the knee. Nathan talked to the foal while he worked and Betsy stroked it.

When the last knot was tied, Dick and Nathan got the shaky foal to her feet and held her up, but when they urged her to walk, she slumped to the ground.

"Betsy, you help Dick hold her up and let me look at her hind legs," Nathan said and squatted down behind the foal. "They are limber, too," he said glumly.

Nathan cut more bark and Dick more shavings. They

wrapped and tied the hind legs. Once more, they stood the foal on her feet. She swayed uncertainly. Belle whinnied trying to jerk loose to come to her foal. The little foal took a tiny step toward her, then stopped and would not try again.

"We'll let it suck, then maybe it will have more strength," Nathan said. "After all, it is not yet a day old and must be all worn out from us handling it so much. Even strong foals sleep most of their time the first few days."

They carried her to Belle and she nuzzled it closely. For the first time, she nursed standing on her own feet, held upright by Nathan.

"She's getting full," Dick bragged. "Her sides are stickin' out!"

Betsy went to Belle stroking her face. "Nathan will make your foal live and she will be a fine one," she said with certainty, "and we'll all love her, every minute."

"I believe she'll be a fine filly," Nathan said as he helped the tired foal lie down by its mother. She folded her knees and curled up as best she could.

Nathan took a long breath. He felt as tired as the foal. "Anyway, she's alive and got a chance," he said gratefully. "I wouldn't feel right if we hadn't tried. You both had a hand in it."

Dick looked up at the sun through a rift of tree branches. "It's nigh four o'clock. I have to go. Ma gets anxious if I'm out after dark."

"Come again, Dick, and much obliged for all the help."

"You're welcome. And I will come again. Maybe we

can go to see Panther Cave. You're about half way between the cave and town. Maybe when Walkfast comes we can do it."

"Can I go too?" Betsy asked. "I've never been in a real cave."

Dick shrugged. "You'd have to wear some of Nathan's britches. In some places it's slick with mud and like a tunnel. You have to worm your way along on your stummick. And after a few feet, it's black as tar. We took along a candle and if the candle goes out that means that's bad air and you better get out."

Betsy shivered and the boys laughed.

They watched as Dick got on his horse and started home. He turned, waved, then disappeared in the forest.

"I like him," Nathan said. "Seems as if I've known him a long time. I'm glad we're no farther away from Navestown."

"I wish we could have lived in the settlement," Betsy said wistfully. "Ma liked it there, too."

"You know Pa would never live in a town," Nathan said. "When we were up on the high bluff, we could look down here in the valley. There are hills on all sides. I think one reason Pa liked it was he thought we'd never have any close neighbors." A wave of homesickness washed over him. For a moment, he was home in Kentucky with all the old, familiar things.

They stood silent for a minute. Back in the woods they could hear faint sounds. "It's Pa and Ma," Betsy said. "Let's go and see what they have picked out."

—≫ CHAPTER 6 ≪—

The land gradually sloped up from the creek until it was six or eight feet higher on the valley floor. Ma picked out a homesite on a little knoll with a towering white oak tree that she wanted left by the side of the house. "It will make shade after the other trees are cut down," she said as if she could imagine the little valley planted to crops and the buildings already finished. They decided on a cabin with a loft overhead for the boys to sleep in.

"As long as neighbors will help hoist the logs we can build it higher," Pa said.

"I want a puncheon floor, Peter. I'd rather wait longer and have a floor. It will be warmer, too," Ma said.

"Are we going to have windows?" Betsy asked.

"One each side the of door downstairs," Pa said, "and

one in each end upstairs. The fireplace will be opposite the door on the north wall. Real lucky to have rocks in the creek to build the fireplace."

They turned back to camp. "Now that I know where the house will be, Nathan, you and I will start in the morning and build us a three-sided shed to use while the house is being built. It can be the stable afterwards. Jesse Nave said there were some bears around so the tarp won't be enough."

"And don't forget the panther you heard yesterday," Betsy added.

"Don't go back in the woods alone, always take Shep," Pa cautioned. "And watch out for timber rattlers."

"And Indians!" Ma said bleakly. "I'd rather meet up with a rattlesnake than an Indian."

"Jesse Nave said most of them have gone on west since the land has been ceded to the government. One called Walkfast, about Dick's age, seems to be friends. His tribe comes through here in the summer to fish and hunt." Pa didn't sound worried.

Ma took hold of Andy's hand. "Just the same I don't understand them."

"Pa," Betsy said, "Nathan got the foal's legs fixed and it stood up and got its dinner."

"I had to steady it a bit," Nathan added, "but it did take one little step. Dick and Betsy helped, too."

"It may live for awhile, but I've never seen an animal get over limberleg," Pa said as he looked at the foal.

Maybe because they never had a chance, Nathan

thought stubbornly, remembering how Pa and Jesse Nave both said the foal should be destroyed.

The foal was still asleep when Nathan untied Belle and turned her loose to find something to eat. She would not go far away.

"Haven't felt any mosquitoes," Pa said. "Maybe they won't be bad with the creek running as swift as it does. There's a breeze, too. It'll get dark early here in the timber with the high cliff to the west, so best get our camp made and pallets fixed and eat a bite before dark."

"I'm going to sleep over by Belle and Trinket, so I can help her during the night," Nathan said and began to cut small leafy limbs for a padding under his quilt.

Pa brought up part of an old dead stump and put it on the fire. "It'll last all night to help keep away the bugs and curious animals."

By dark they had eaten and with support from Nathan the foal had nursed again. Now everyone was bedded down for the night. The little campfire made darting shadows, lighting the blackness that walled them in. Soft, murmuring sounds came from the running creek.

It was like many camps they had made on the long journey from Kentucky, yet it was completely different. This was where they would build a cabin. Good or bad, this would be their home. Nathan looked up trying to see the stars, but only one showed through the thick canopy of leaves. Not far away a whippoorwill began its lonely song and Nathan reached out to touch the little foal. She felt cold and shivery so Nathan put part of his quilt over her.

By the creek a frog began to croak. The crickets fiddled. Belle made a soft, fluttery sound to the foal and Nathan drifted off to sleep.

Later, Nathan suddenly came awake. The foal was struggling to get up and Belle was tramping restlessly, her head thrown up, eyes staring into the darkness. Shep stared into the darkness, too, growling deep in his throat, hair standing up along his back. Nathan raised upon his elbow and looked across the fire into the darkness. Two red eyes shone in the firelight, so low to the ground Nathan thought it must be a wolf or a panther.

Belle snorted pawing the ground, then the gleaming eyes were gone. There was a sound from the tarpaulin. Pa was awake. "I expect it was the smell of the new foal," Pa said softly. "Stir up the fire, Nathan."

Nathan stirred the fire and Shep stopped growling. Belle was still uneasy. Nathan helped the foal to its feet. She stood alone to nurse, but Nathan kept his hands near, should it slump. Belle nuzzled it and nickered softly, watching the darkness as she licked the foal. Nathan watched, too, shivers running down his back, but the gleaming eyes were gone.

Suddenly Trinket butted her mother and took three little staggering steps all by herself! Nathan wanted to shout! Belle nickered anxiously and stepped between the foal and the forest. "She isn't going to run away," Nathan said softly, "but she will live. Oh Belle, the splints work!"

The foal slumped awkwardly and Nathan caught it as it went down. She stretched out on her side and went to sleep. Nathan stretched out beside her and pulled up the quilt, one hand resting on the foal. Up above an owl hooted. Far away came the lonely cry of a wolf. Shep stood close. "You're a good dog," Nathan whispered. "Watch camp. Don't let anything get us." He gave the dog another pat and was soon asleep.

After Nathan awakened, Pa stirred the fire and Ma fried some hominy Mrs. Nave had given them. Shadows were deep in the valley, but high above, the first sunlight was edging the top of the cliff.

"Your foal is better," Ma said and smiled at Nathan. "She almost got up awhile ago. I think she's hungry."

"She is better," Nathan agreed. "She took three steps all by herself in the night. Come on, Trinket, let's have breakfast." With a little nudging and helping from Nathan the foal got to her feet and walked four, stiff, staggering little steps to her mother. Then she began to drink.

"Did you see that?" Nathan exulted. "Another time and she can do it alone. She is going to walk!"

Ma smiled at Nathan, but Pa said nothing. Even if the foal was stronger, Nathan knew it was only the splints that were letting her walk, but Trinket was only two days old. Nathan took the plate Ma handed him and began to eat. The hominy was good. Mrs. Nave had shared the wild honey, too, which made the cornpone taste fine. "We'll have to find us a bee tree of our own," Pa said as he spread honey on the pone. "Sweetnin' sure makes things taste better." With a bit of crust he wiped the last bit of honey from his plate.

"Nathan, you bring up some water for your mother while I sharpen the axes. Betsy, I'd like you to come along and bring a firebrand with you. I want to get the shed built before it rains."

Nathan untied Belle to turn her loose. "You'll keep an eye on the foal, won't you, Ma?"

"Yes, don't worry."

As they walked over to the chosen spot, Pa cut off all the low-hanging tree branches along the way, but many of the trees were so tall, the lowest branches were far over Pa's head.

Pa chose a spot where no big trees would have to be cut. It was on lower ground than the homesite and about a hundred feet north. Pa walked around through the woods and marked the trees they would use, most of them about ten or twelve inches through at the butt.

"I'll cut down the trees, measure, and top them," Pa said as he took off his shirt. "You can do the trimming. Limbs big enough for Ma to burn at camp, cut into short lengths; the others we'll pile and burn."

Pa spit on his hands, rubbed them together and picked up the axe and began to chop. The muscles on his back grew shiny with sweat and chips flew as the axe bit into the trunk. Soon there was a deep gash on each side. The tree shook and slowly toppled. Pa measured five lengths of his axe handle from the bottom of the tree trunk, then he cut through it again.

"Now it's your turn," Pa said to Nathan as he leaned against a tree to rest.

Nathan began to trim the branches from the log, cutting them close. Soon he had a little pile of firewood and a bigger pile of small limbs and leaves to burn. Betsy, wearing a pair of Nathan's breeches, came with a piece of burning wood and soon had a fire going, but the blaze was almost smothered when she piled on the green branches and leaves. A cloud of smoke slowly floated up and was lost in the tops of the tall trees.

So it went.

By the middle of the morning, Nathan stopped to go back to camp to get the foal up to nurse. Andy came running. "Nathan, Trinket got up all by herself, almost. She had an awful time, but Ma pushed and she made it!"

Nathan looked at the foal now lying down again.

"Nathan, she did get up almost by herself. I only pushed a little. In a few days I think she can get up and down alone."

"Ma, you do think she will live, don't you?"

"She's getting stronger, but what will happen when you take off the bark, I don't know."

Nathan felt down deep inside that the foal would live and walk. She was his first patient. She had to live!

At noon they rested, Pa stretched out flat on the ground. "Marthy," he said, "we got seven logs down and by quitting time it will be twelve. That's almost half enough. Day after tomorrow I think we can start laying up the shed."

"You'll have to take time to go hunting soon, Pa. The side meat is almost gone."

After dinner Ma said she would help with the foal and Nathan wouldn't need to come back.

Pa judged it was four o'clock when the twelfth log was finished. He trimmed it himself and helped Betsy pile the limbs on the fire. Betsy and Nathan were so tired they had long ago stopped talking and even Pa was quiet as they walked back to camp. Andy had eaten and was asleep on his pallet. As soon as the foal was fed, Nathan ate, spread out his quilt by the foal and was asleep by dark, too tired to look for a star.

—≫ CHAPTER 7 ≪—

ours later, Nathan was awakened by a clap of thunder that jerked him from the ground. Flashes of lightning made the camp like day. A crashing roar filled the air.

"Nathan!" Pa yelled. "It's a bad one coming. Drive the tarp pegs tighter!"

Nathan stumbled up, got his axe and drove the pegs down. Ma got up and turned the cooking pot over the coals of fire. Pa tightened the rope between the trees. Belle was standing over the foal, the mules and horses near her.

A sudden blinding blue light cracked and split the air, rocking the ground under their feet. "That was a close one!" Pa shouted. "Smell the brimstone!"

They huddled close together under the tarp. It bellied up and down and the tree bent in the fury. One limb broke off crashing near the camp. Pa held Andy in his arms with

Ma standing close against him. Betsy stuck her fingers in her ears and hid her eyes against Ma's shoulder. Nathan shivered as streaks of lightning snapped and cracked overhead. Shep whimpered against his legs. Nathan reached down and picked him up, holding him tight. The rain fell in torrents, beating and lashing the trees, but finally it moved on, leaving the camp soaked and the creek roaring.

There were coals under the kettle still and Pa managed to get a blaze going by the charred log. Trinket was wet and shivering and Belle was licking her. Nathan rubbed her and got her to nurse. The horses and mules stayed near camp for awhile then went away, Major's bell tinkling in the darkness.

"It's coming daylight," Pa said pointing up to the high cliff where a rim of light was etched against the sky. "About four o'clock. Ma, let's have a bite to eat and we'll get an early start on the logs."

Betsy groaned. Nathan felt as if he could never trim another tree. His shoulder ached and there was a blister on his right hand. He was cold and wet and miserable. Oh, why would his father want to come out to this wilderness when he could have stayed in Kentucky? He wished he had never heard of Missouri!

Ma warmed up the cornpone, boiled some water in the bucket and poured each tin cup full of the steaming liquid. Then she opened one of the boxes and from some secret place brought out a little packet of tea and put a pinch in each cup.

"Oh, Ma!" Betsy cried out. "That's the best tea I ever tasted. You do the nicest things! Maybe I'll live now!" She reached for her mother and kissed her.

"That was nicer than the tea," Ma said softly.

"Well, if I didn't have work to do, I'd play a tune on the fiddle just to celebrate the tea party; but by the time we get to the trees, it will be full daylight—already sunup on the cliff."

Ma filled each cup again with hot water, reusing the tea leaves.

"Tastes almost as good the second time," Nathan declared, as he drained the cup.

"Chances are it won't storm again for a few days and we can get the shed done. Then I'll get some meat and find a bee tree," Pa said.

"Don't wait too long," Ma cautioned. "Takes strength to get things done and the side meat is about gone."

Pa picked up his axe and the rifle, and Nathan followed along behind with his own axe. Betsy would come later.

Underneath the ashes, the fire was still alive and Nathan stirred it into a blaze before beginning to trim the waiting logs. It was the middle of the forenoon when they heard a man shout from the camp.

"What's a stranger doing out here?" Pa said, a puzzled frown on his face. "I'd better go see." He leaned his axe against a log. As he moved to pick up the rifle, another shout sounded nearer. Soon Mr. Lamson came into sight, a downcast look on his round face. Pa welcomed him, inviting him to sit down on a log.

"Quite a storm we had last night," Pa said, after a few moments.

"Yes, it was," Mr. Lamson agreed bleakly, not looking at Pa. Something was terribly wrong, Nathan knew, besides the storm.

"Lightnin' split a big oak right up on the trail," Pa tried again.

"Saw it," Mr. Lamson said absently and Pa did not say any more.

Finally, Mr. Lamson heaved a deep sigh. "Guess you are wonderin' why I came," he said slowly, and Pa nodded. "It was the storm last night finally did it," he began. "Maybe the Naves told you we've had bad luck, lost two little girls, one two years old last year and the baby this spring. Mary, that's my wife, just can't get over it. A new country is hard on woman folks. . . She just can't see anything good here and wants to go back to Ohio where our folks live. I want to stay, but the lightning hit a tree right by our house last night and that seemed to be the final straw. Mary just lost her mind and screamed and screamed. So I gave in and said we'd go back to Ohio. Can't do nothin' nor have any peace when your woman's in such misery."

"That's so," Pa agreed. "But people die and lightning strikes in Ohio, too, Mr. Lamson. Just going back there won't keep Mary from having troubles."

"Being with her folks will help," Nathan said. Pa gave him a stern look for speaking up. Nathan, embarrassed, looked away, but in the silence that followed, he thought resentfully that it was too bad, all the same, that Pa didn't seem to care so much about Ma's feelings as Mr. Lamson did his wife's.

Clearly Mr. Lamson had something else on his mind. At last, he swallowed hard and spoke with an effort, "Jesse Nave is buying the homestead of forty acres. He told me you said you would trade one or both horses for a cow or two. . . I need another team and I got two good cows, but one's dry now. I got some pigs and chickens and ducks and maybe some other things you'll probably need to get started. I thought maybe we could do some swappin'." Mr. Lamson looked at Pa and sighed again.

Nathan felt a lump in his throat. This was real trouble. Ohio was as far away as Kentucky. He thought of the long miles the Lamsons had to go. Ma didn't want to come to Missouri, but like Mrs. Lamson, she was here . . . all on account of Pa.

"Going horseback or in a wagon?" Pa asked.

"In a wagon. Jesse Nave is going to take his flatboat down to St. Louis. I'm going to build a raft to tie on behind the boat to carry most of the hides. That will give room for our wagon and horses on the boat. Be a big help. I cut some off the price of the land. Jesse Nave is a good man to know when you're in trouble," he said with conviction.

It was quiet again and Nathan heard the cry of a mourning dove.

Pa chewed on a twig and pondered. "I want to keep the mules," he said, "but I'll swap you one or both horses for a cow and other things. My wife rode a bay gelding all the way from Kentucky. He's gentle and strong, a 4-year old.

We call him Charlie. The other one my daughter rode, a spotted gelding, gentle as they come. He's Spot. Nathan, see if you can whistle up the horses."

Nathan gave a long piercing whistle as he started to the camp.

"Come, help me find the horses," he said to Betsy. "Pa's going to swap Charlie and maybe Spot to Mr. Lamson. They are going to Ohio. Mrs. Lamson had a fit last night when it stormed."

"Poor soul," Ma said. "I really can't blame her with all their trouble, but I hate to see Charlie and Spot start for Ohio when they just came all those awful miles from Kentucky."

"I'm not going with you!" Betsy cried out. "I don't want Spot sold to Mr. Lamson!"

"Mr. Lamson will be good to him," Nathan said as he got the halters.

"Take a little salt with you," Ma said and measured a precious spoonful into a tin cup.

Betsy shook her head and would not go, so Nathan went alone. He did not blame Betsy for crying. She thought almost as much of Spot as he did of Belle. He followed the creek north, whistling every few minutes, then listening. He had not gone far when he heard Major's bell and knew the horses were coming. He held out some salt in the palm of his hand and Charlie and Spot came and he slipped the halters on them. "I feel like a Judas," he thought as they crowded close to get the salt. The mules did not come.

He started back to camp, Major following. Pa and Mr.

Lamson were waiting and Pa took Charlie's halter. "Sound as a new kettle, gentle, willing to do more than his share."

Mr. Lamson looked in Charlie's mouth, felt of his legs, stood back and sized him up. Betsy stood at the tarp her face swollen from crying. Ma stood beside her holding Andy by the hand.

Pa turned to Spot. "Same age as Charlie and just as gentle, my daughter rode him from Kentucky. Not quite as heavy as Charlie."

Mr. Lamson looked at the horses, then at Betsy and back again. "We leave in four days," he finally said. "I'd like to keep the cow until the day we go, if you don't mind. The cow is the one thing my wife hates to leave behind. I'll take Charlie and think about Spot. Don't want another woman crying over something I've done."

"I'll bring him in the day after tomorrow and look at the cow and other things," Pa answered.

"See you then," Mr. Lamson replied and got on his horse without a backward glance, his shoulders sagging.

Pa turned to Betsy. "I'm sorry about Spot, but we need other things more than we need Spot. If I don't swap him to Mr. Lamson, I'll sell or trade him to somebody else."

"Then sell him to me! Pa, I've got the five dollar gold piece Grandpa gave me. Take it Pa! I'd a heap rather have Spot than the gold piece! It's in Ma's reticule!"

Pa's face reddened and he looked at Betsy, then at Charlie and Spot.

"It sounds like a fair trade to me," Ma said clearly and looked at Pa.

"I don't think you could do any better," Nathan spoke up.

"Well, I do tell! Three against one. I never thought it of you!" Pa shut his lips firmly.

Then Ma laughed, Betsy giggled and Nathan joined in. Suddenly, Pa's face broke into a smile. "I guess I sold a horse. Betsy, he's yours for five dollars."

Betsy grabbed Pa and kissed him and then kissed Spot.

Pa looked up at the sun, "It's close to dinner time. Ma, if there's any cornpone left from breakfast, let's have a piece and we'll go back to making logs."

─── ⊰ CHAPTER 8 ⊱ ───

Aﬀter breakfast Pa was ready to leave for Navestown by sunup. Major was saddled and Charlie haltered. Ma stroked Charlie's face telling him he was a good horse and she hoped the road to Ohio was not too rough. Nathan and Betsy rubbed him and Betsy cried. They watched until Pa and the horses were out of sight. When they disappeared up the trail, Belle gave a high, lonely whinny as if knowing she would never see Charlie again. Spot nickered and nickered.

Nathan felt his throat tighten and he went over to Belle and Trinket and the lonesomeness swept over him.

High above, the cliff was etched with sunlight, but the valley was still thick with shadows. Nathan wondered if he would ever stop hungering for their home in Kentucky. Here, he had no time to read in the doctor book. How would he ever get to be a doctor? He sighed and his shoulders slumped.

Ma poked the fire. "Let's all work and clean up the camp and get ready to wash some clothes."

"Oh Ma," Betsy wailed. "Let's go fishing. Yesterday when we looked for the horses, we saw a deep pool in the creek with fish in it. Maybe we could catch a mess for supper. Ma, do we have to wash clothes today?"

Ma looked down at the fire and Nathan felt his heart ache. His mother looked pale and thin. She had never really gotten over the sick spell in Illinois. "Let the washing go, Ma," Nathan urged. "Let's all go! I'll cut some poles and we can find some worms. It won't hurt to wear our clothes one more day."

Ma looked up and laughed. For a moment she looked almost as young as Betsy. "You're right, Nathan, and a hundred years from now none of us will know the difference."

Suddenly it was a fine day! Nathan got the hooks and lines and cut some poles. Ma gave Andy some breakfast and Betsy put some cornpone in a cloth. Ma put on a shirt and breeches of Pa's, so she wouldn't tear her skirts on the briers.

Nathan gave the foal a boost so it could stand up and drink its breakfast and untied Belle so she could forage. They were ready to go. Shep ran ahead, but Nathan called him back. "Shep, you can't go. Stay and watch the camp." Shep wilted and he came slowly back to camp. "Next time," Nathan promised and gave him a pat as they left.

It was quite a procession. Nathan led the way, carrying his rifle, the lines and fishhooks in his pocket and worms in a piece of sacking. Ma and Andy came behind him, carrying the cornpone and Betsy with the poles bringing up the rear.

They followed the creek and in a little open spot found a patch of wild blackberries. They picked and ate every ripe one. After cornpone and side meat, Nathan decided, nothing had ever tasted so good. Farther on they found another patch. "Let's save these for supper and pick them as we go home," Ma said.

"Ah, Ma," Nathan looked at them longingly. "What if I die before suppertime?"

"Then I'll eat your share," Betsy giggled.

They found the deep pool around the second bend in the creek. While Betsy tied on the lines, Nathan baited the hooks and soon had their lines in the water. The creek flowed at the foot of the cliff and the pool was dark and clear.

Mom was helping Andy throw out his line when Nathan suddenly felt a pull and the float went under. He gave a jerk and landed a shining silver sunperch about the size of his hand. "Look!" he boasted. "I caught the first one! A sunperch is good eating."

"I caught one, too!" Betsy sang out. "And it's bigger than yours!" Two fish were flopping on the bank.

"Ma, use my line while I put the fish on a stringer. This is the best fishing I ever saw!" Nathan pulled a length of line from his pocket and strung the fish and put them back in the water, tying the line to a bush that leaned over the creek. "We'll sure have fish for supper. Look at that! Ma, you caught one, too!"

It seemed to Nathan he didn't have time to catch another fish because he was so busy stringing. Finally sixteen fish were on the stringer and the biting slowed down.

"Probably the first time this pool was ever fished," Ma said, "and the fish aren't wary. We'll clean them before we go home, so it won't draw flies to the camp."

Andy began rummaging in the cloth for cornpone. "I'm hungry, I want to eat," he said.

"Let's all eat," Betsy and Ma agreed and handed out the pone.

"My, it seems good not to have anything to do for awhile," Nathan said as he stretched out on a flat rock. "This is a fine spot."

"It's not far from camp," Ma said, "with fish to catch and blackberries to pick, some of us will come often."

"That will be me," Betsy said. "Nathan has to help with the shed."

"You have to burn leaves," Nathan said shortly.

"Never mind," Ma warned, "we all have to work and get as much done as possible before winter sets in. It'll be a lot colder here than it was in Kentucky."

They caught three more fish then Ma said it was time to clean them and start home. It was a nice catch and there would be enough for everyone to have his fill.

Nathan took a last look at the pool as he picked up his rifle and they started back. When they came to the blackberry patch, Ma spread out the cloth that had held the cornpone. "We'll use this to hold the berries. And don't you children eat all you pick. We want to surprise your Pa."

Soon there was quite a pile of berries on the white cloth and Betsy went to the other side of the patch to pick. Suddenly there was the chilling buzz of a rattlesnake and Nathan froze at the sound.

"What's that noise?" Andy asked looking at Nathan.

"Hush! Don't move. Don't move, Andy. That's a bad, bad snake," Nathan said through stiff lips.

"It's here, Nathan, here." Nathan could barely hear Betsy say the words.

"Don't anybody but Nathan move. Andy, stand still!" Ma said evenly.

Nathan stepped carefully for his rifle and began to pick his way toward Betsy, trying not to make a sound. The timber rattler was coiled, not more than three feet from Betsy, its head raised ready to strike. It was a big one and any sudden movement might make it strike. Across the blackberry patch, Ma spoke softly. "Don't move, Betsy, Nathan is going to shoot. He will kill the snake."

A clammy chill of fear swept over Nathan, but his hands held steady as he raised the rifle and sighted for the snake's head. He was close enough to see the rattles vibrate and make the warning sound, but they were so near the color of the dead grass and spots of shade he could hardly focus on them. He held his breath, squeezed the trigger and the snake was writhing at Betsy's feet.

Betsy burst into tears, her face white as chalk with strain. "Oh, Nathan," she sobbed, "I was afraid you'd miss!"

"I knew he wouldn't," Ma said, her face as white as Betsy's.

Nathan felt weak and he shivered as he bent over the big timber rattler. It's head was sheared off cleanly by the bullet. He got out his hunting knife and cut off the rattles. "Twelve rattles and a button," he said in amazement. "It's big around as my arm!"

"Let's go," Ma said. "We've enough berries for supper. Leave the snake there. It's mate may be near. Folks say a dead snake drives other snakes away."

Shep barked and came to meet them, running back and forth to camp. "Everything all right?" Nathan reached down to pet him. "Did you look after Trinket?"

Shep would not wait to be petted, but ran back to camp and Nathan felt a sudden, horrible sinking in his stomach as he broke into a run. Something had happened. His mouth felt dry as linsey when he got to camp. His eyes searched, but everything seemed in place; then he glanced at the place where Trinket always slept by her mother. The foal was gone!

Shep barked and ran on the path toward the homesite. Nathan ran after him. Half-way, he heard Belle nicker. Looking proud and wise, she stood beside a clump of bushes with Trinket beside her. The foal's eyes were round and shining as she stood close to her mother, her brush of a tail switching back and forth.

"You little stinker," Nathan panted. "You think you're smart, don't you? Walking clear over here." He stroked her face and ran his hand down her back. "Well, I think you're smart, too. I guess now you can go anywhere. But Belle, you have to bring her back to camp at night," Nathan cautioned. "Panthers or wolves might get her, or maybe a bear!"

He looked at the bark around the foal's legs and the hickory strings were holding. Everything was fine now, but would the bones grow strong so that she would walk like other colts? "I will not worry," Nathan said determinedly. "Her bones will strengthen."

He met Betsy running, all out of breath. "Trinket?" she panted.

Nathan grinned. "Trinket is all right. She walked all the way over here and is still standing up."

"Oh Nathan, I was so afraid something had happened."

Nathan grinned at his sister, "So was I and Shep knew something wasn't right." He reached down and patted the dog. "Good dog," he said and started toward camp.

It was getting dusk and Ma was uneasy until they heard a cow bell and Pa singing. "Get the fish from the creek, Nathan," Ma said as she put some grease in the skillet. "Betsy, you wash the berries. My, won't we have a surprise for your Pa?"

Major was ahead, then Pa leading the cow. Major's saddle was out of sight beneath things Pa had traded from the Lamsons or they had given him.

The cow was a yellow brindle with little curved horns. She eyed them across the fire and seemed tame as a kitten. "Mrs. Lamson said her name is Molly. She cried when I started away and asked that we please treat her well. I promised her we would. She gives about half a gallon a day and is to have a calf in November." Pa smiled looking at Ma and Betsy. "She has always been milked by a woman." Molly's eyes were big and round as she looked at them and then at the fire. They all gathered around to pet her.

Pa began unloading. Everyone watched to see what he had brought. It was like Christmas and Ma put off frying the fish and looked, too.

There were gourds of different sizes, seeds tied up in a cloth, a pail of honey and a sack of cornmeal. A tin bucket with earthen jars stuck in it and an old buffalo robe. A jar of homemade lye for making soap and a big gourdful of grease. "Mrs. Lamson said she was getting ready to make soap, but had no time for it now, so she sent the makins' to you."

"I bought her spinning wheel and her big kettle and left them in the house until I go back next time. They almost gave the things away for no room in the wagon." Pa shook his head. "Bad time, nobody glad to go but Mrs. Lamson. She never even looked back."

"Poor Mrs. Lamson," Ma said and began frying the fish. It was feast with enough crusty fish for everyone and hot cornpone topped with honey and for a grand finish, blackberries with milk.

They told Pa about the rattlesnake and Nathan took

the rattles from his pocket. Pa looked at them silently. "Jesse Nave warned me, but said the snakes were thicker up on the cliffs and among the rocks where it was sunny." He handed the rattles back to Nathan. "Better give them to your sister for a keepsake."

Nathan hesitated, then handed them to Betsy.

Later Nathan stretched out on his pallet. Through the branches of the tree he could see the twinkle of a star. Sometime in the night he felt Trinket against his back. He put out his hand to pat her and went back to sleep.

—➤ CHAPTER 9 ⬅—

N athan and Pa began building the shed early the next morning. They dug holes for the corners and set four poles upright. Then they began laying the walls. Nathan hooked a rope around a log and hitched Sam to it and pulled the log to the site. It was slow hard work, but by night the three walls were six logs high.

"Seven logs high will be enough," Pa said at quitting time. "Unless it rains, I think we can get it roofed tomorrow and get the bark shingles on the next day. You're good help, Son," Pa said as they started to camp. "Almost as good as a man, bettern' some."

Nathan mumbled his thanks, too tired to care. He hardly remembered when he went to bed and it seemed only an instant until Pa was shaking him. "Son, time to get up. Ma's got breakfast ready. Got to finish the shed today."

Nathan put on his shoes and got up, going to the creek to wash his face. Trinket went part way with him.

"With Molly such a pet and Belle and Trinket, we'll never get lonesome," Ma said as they ate breakfast.

By evening the log roof was on and the sky still clear. But the next day was cloudy threatening rain, the air sultry. Pa and Nathan and Betsy worked all day. Pa cut bark on the tree trunks. Nathan and Betsy loosened it with knives and peeled it off. Before the bark curled, Pa laid the pieces on top of the log roof like shingles and weighted each row down with a sapling held flat with a rock at each end.

Right after dinner, Ma began moving the lighter weight things from the camp to the shed. Even Andy carried spoons and tin cups. She also moved some of the live coals and started a cooking fire in front of the open side of the shed.

"Nathan, you ditch the shed while I finish the shingles. It's going to rain for sure," Pa said. Nathan hurried to dig a shallow ditch around the building to keep the water from running inside. Before he finished, thunder rumbled overhead, but it only sprinkled. The storm went around to the east.

"Tomorrow I'll fasten the tarp to the roof so that it can be let down in front to keep out the rain when it comes from the south," Pa said.

"My, I'm thankful to have this shelter," Ma said. "I feel safe from everything except rattlesnakes and Indians."

Pa smiled. "Jesse Nave says the Indians aren't quarrelsome and the rattlesnakes always give warning. But don't anyone ever go back in the woods without the hoe. After awhile we'll get some of the poisonous snakes killed off and the others don't matter."

Ma said quietly, "They all matter to me."

Nathan went to bed right after supper, while his mother and father talked by the fire.

It was barely daylight when Nathan awakened to the smell of frying side meat. Pa had just come from the creek with a bucket of water. "The horses and mules were up at the old camp when I went for water," Pa said. "Guess they feel safer where humans have been. Wish I had a fence to protect them. The wolves howled last night." Pa sighed, "Can't get everything done at once."

Nathan pulled on his boots and went to the fire.

"Nathan, your Ma and I talked last night and decided I should go to the Land Office at Lexington to enter forty acres of land. If I wait until the cabin is done, it will be winter. Jesse Nave said more people were coming into the country and somebody might take a-liking to this very spot. Now, Son, that means you'll have to take care of things while I'm gone."

Nathan was suddenly wide awake. "How . . . how long will it take you?"

"Maybe two weeks, maybe less. I talked with Lamson; he went a year ago, said it took him two weeks, but the trail should be better now. There's lots of bee trees in the river bottom and wagons have been coming up from Lexington, loading up with barrels of honey. From the village of Chillicothe, the trail should be better, but it's mostly through thick timber like we had from Brunswick.

"What you want I should do?" Nathan asked, his heart sinking. What if someone got bit with a rattlesnake? What if a bear came into camp? What if Ma got sick? A thousand things raced through his mind.

"Just do the best you can each day," Pa said. "That's all anybody could do. I'm going out this morning and look for a deer. We'll make jerky and with fish from the creek, you'll get along. If you have to, you can get some meat, bad as you hate to kill things."

Nathan flushed. Pa always seemed to find a tender place. "If it's to eat that's reason enough," he said quietly.

Pa was gone several hours, but he brought back a young buck slung across his shoulders. He dressed it and cut out a big roast and put it on to cook in the kettle. The rest of it Pa cut into real thin strips and hung it over the fire to make jerky. It would dry out and have a smoky flavor. It was the only way they could keep fresh meat in the summer.

In the afternoon Nathan and Betsy went to the blackberry patch. "I'm afraid," Betsy said. "What if that old snake had a mate, or maybe a lot of kin?"

"We'll make a loud noise," Nathan answered. "That will scare them away, but watch where you step."

They shouted and yelled, following the trail and came to the patch of vines full of dark ripe berries. They began picking and eating. "It's easier to carry them back this way than in the bucket." Nathan grinned and put a ripe berry in his mouth.

Finally the patch was picked clean of ripe ones and the

bucket almost full. "And we didn't see a single rattler," Betsy said thankfully as they started home.

Supper was a feast with fresh venison and blackberries and milk, with cornpone and honey.

"I staked Major out so I wouldn't have to hunt him in the morning. Nathan, it's best to tie Molly up every night until she gets used to staying here. And, Son, I marked some trees for the cabin. Try to cut and trim one or more every day. That will be a big help toward getting it built. With fish and jerky, there should be enough to eat. I won't be gone over two weeks and I hope to get home sooner than that."

"What about Indians?" Ma asked.

"I can't answer, but be friendly and if they want victuals, give them all they want. Too bad I have to leave you, Marthy, but I'll get back just as soon as I can; then we'll have our land. We're lucky we sold the place in Kentucky for enough to pay for the homestead here."

Everyone went to bed early, but it was a long time before Nathan went to sleep.

It was still dark when he awakened. Pa was eating and Ma had wrapped some of the driest jerky and cornpone in a cloth for him to take on the journey. Nathan got up, wishing with all his heart that Pa did not have to go.

Pa put his hand on Nathan's shoulder. "You take care, Son, 'till I get back."

Nathan tried to sound brave and convincing, but the words were hard to say, "Pa, don't you worry. We'll be all right."

Pa kissed Ma goodby and swung into the saddle. They watched until horse and rider disappeared into the darkness and the night was still.

"We might as well go back to bed and get some more sleep," Ma said. "Be a long time until morning."

Sometime during the night, Trinket had come to bed and Nathan lay down beside her again and faced the fire. Shep sat up and stared into the darkness, listening. He came to Nathan and whined softly. "I know," Nathan said. "Pa's gone, but he'll be back."

Nathan tried to go back to sleep, but every little sound alerted him. Far away a lonely whippoorwill called out, and over by the high bluff, another answered. In the distance, a wolf howled and gooseflesh popped out along Nathan's arms. Shep whined uneasily and the flickering shadows from the fire seemed alive. A clammy fear knotted Nathan's stomach. What if some terrible thing happened while Pa was gone?

He swallowed the lump in his throat and stared into the fire and gradually it faded out. The next thing he heard was Molly's muffled bell and the sound of a stream of milk hitting the bottom of an empty bucket. The sun was slanting through the treetops. Ma was milking. Nathan threw back the quilt and got to his feet, ashamed he had overslept. This sure wasn't taking Pa's place.

—⇒ CHAPTER 10 ⇐—

The morning after Pa left, Nathan felled two trees and trimmed them, piling the limbs on the ashes of the old fire. That afternoon he chopped down another and trimmed it.

"If I can cut down three a day and Pa is gone two weeks, not counting Sundays, that will be thirty-six trees. Pa figured it would take about a hundred logs for the sides and the gable ends," Nathan said as they ate supper.

"If the logs are all cut and trimmed, then when the neighbors come to help, it will go up in a hurry," Ma said, and Nathan knew she would be thankful to have a house again.

"Best of all," Ma went on, "we'll have a cleared spot to plant some garden, even if it will be late."

"And the lilac bushes," Betsy said, "one slip has two new leaves on it."

It was barely dark when they went to bed. Nathan

moved his quilt over in front of the shed where Pa slept and put his rifle within reach. Belle and the foal nosed around where Nathan usually slept, then Trinket came over, snuffled at Nathan and got down beside him.

At the back of the shed, Betsy laughed. "Now if Belle and Spot and Molly and the mules would come to sleep with us, it would be just like living in the Ark."

Between the shed and the fire, Shep lay on guard watching the darkness. Nathan wondered how far Pa had traveled and where he was sleeping tonight. Once he awoke and the fire was only a glow of coals beside the charred log. The darkness seemed thick and close as a blanket. Nathan raised up and listened. Shep got up and walked around the fire then came back to Nathan. Behind him Ma moved and Nathan knew she was awake. "Ma, Shep says everything is all right," he told her softly. He reached out a hand to Trinket and went to sleep.

The next morning Molly's bell woke them early. "She's better than a rooster," Nathan grumbled as he got up and put wood on the fire. He looked longingly at his pallet, then picked up the water bucket and went to the creek. Ma was milking when he came back. It was going to be a hot day.

It was the middle of the forenoon and Nathan had just finished trimming his first tree, when Shep growled and ran up the path toward the shed. Nathan picked up his rifle and hurried up the path behind the dog.

A cold knot twisted in the pit of his stomach when he saw three Indians standing in front of the shed talking to Ma and Betsy. They all turned toward Nathan as he walked up. Ma's face was as white as her Sunday kerchief and Betsy seemed paralyzed. Andy was holding to Ma's skirt.

"Be still, Shep," Nathan said. The Indians eyed Nathan's rifle and looked at him warily. They did not have guns, only hunting knives stuck in their belts. They seemed about his age.

The one wearing leather breeches spoke to Nathan. "We want to see colt with bark legs. Dick told us."

"You're Walkfast!" Nathan said, letting out a long breath. "He's told me about you."

The Indian nodded and a faint smile shone on his face.

"I'm Nathan. This is my mother and my sister and brother." The Indian boys looked at Ma and Betsy, but said nothing.

Nathan hesitated as the Indians waited. Jesse Nave said all the Indians around these parts were friendly, but would they be friendly to him? Were more back in the woods waiting for him to leave and then come to the camp? Should he leave Ma and Betsy and Andy alone to find the foal? He dared not seem unfriendly. There were three of them to one of him.

He looked at Ma's white face and tried to smile as he handed her the rifle. "Come on," he said to Walkfast. "The foal is not far from here." He started back the way he had come. The Indians walked behind him and he could feel their nearness, hear their soft footsteps. Shep followed behind, rumbling in his throat.

Belle was eating leaves from the tree Nathan had felled. She looked up and whinnied when she saw them. The foal sidled up against her, eyeing the strangers. Nathan went to her and stroked her neck. "They came to see your foal," he said soothingly.

Belle looked at the strangers and stepped between them and her foal. But Trinket was curious and walked around her mother sticking out her nose sniffing the strangers, bright eyes questioning. Nathan spoke to her and held out his hand and Trinket came to him. The Indian boys chuckled as the foal walked in her stiff, awkward way. They pointed at the foal's legs then came close to look. Belle fretted, tossing her head, nickering to the foal as two of the boys squatted down to look. But Nathan held her off. Shep was uneasy, too, walking around them, bristles raised along his back.

Walkfast turned to Nathan. "I'll tell the Old One about the bark, she would want to know."

Nathan nodded and smiled. Then he released his hold on Belle and she took the foal away. The Indian boys watched and Trinket tried to show off and kicked up her heels, her bark-wrapped legs sticking up in the air. The boys bent over laughing and Nathan laughed too. It was the first time Trinket had ever tried that.

"We go now," Walkfast said to Nathan. They started up the path toward the shed Nathan following. It was near dinnertime when they reached the shed, a good odor came from the pot over the fire and one of the boys pointed to it with an eating motion.

Ma looked at Nathan, her face still white. "Is there enough?" he asked.

"For them," Ma said. "We can wait."

"Eat with us," Nathan said to Walkfast and they looked pleased. Ma put spoonfuls of stew on plates and Betsy put on pieces of cornpone beside the stew. The boys squatted on the ground and began eating.

Andy stood for a minute watching. "I want some, too," he demanded, and held out his hand.

They all laughed and a little color came back into Ma's face. She put a spoonful on a plate with a chunk of pone and handed it to Andy. He squatted down just like the Indians and began eating. Walkfast looked at Nathan, a puzzled frown on his face. Then held out his plate toward Nathan's mother. "For Nathan," he said. For the first time Ma smiled. She put another spoonful of stew and a chunk of pone on Walkfast's plate then watched as the Indian squatted beside Nathan and they both began to eat.

The boys ate until the pot was empty. As they got up and started away, Walkfast turned to Nathan, rubbed his stomach, "Good," he said and smiled. "I'll tell Dick about the bark legs." They turned and went away.

When they were out of sight, Betsy let out a long whistling breath. "Whew . . . but I'm glad that's over! I thought I'd faint! What will Pa say when he hears?" She flopped down on the ground.

Ma sat limply on a stump, the spoon still in her hand. "I'll never be so afraid of Indians again. Walkfast is your friend," she said to Nathan. "He wanted you to eat, too."

"Dick thinks Walkfast is a fine person," Nathan said. "They have roamed all over these hills together." He got up to go back to chopping. "Which would you rather have, Ma, the rifle or Shep?"

"I'd rather have Shep. If he barks, then you come running with the rifle."

"I'll cut the trees Pa marked that are the nearest. Betsy, you yell. I could hear that a mile."

Betsy made a face.

Nathan grinned and went back to his tree chopping. Maybe, if he worked late, he could cut two more. He had set his mark at three a day and he wanted to keep it. He leaned his rifle against the closest tree and began to chop, stopping often to listen.

That evening Nathan put salt on the stump by the old camp. The mules and Spot came back each night as they would to a barn and the salt helped to bring them. Molly roamed in the day, but came back in the evening to be milked, and Nathan tied her for the night. Belle stayed near the shed where Trinket slept by Nathan.

As they settled for the night Nathan could see the North Star where a tree had been chopped down and left a vacant place. It was only two days since Pa left, but it seemed a week.

He stirred at every little sound and Shep walked back and forth beyond the firelight. Were there Indians near? Some not as friendly as Walkfast?

Several times he awakened during the night, raised up and looked around and listened. Ma was awake every time. "Have you ever been asleep?" Nathan asked once.

"No," Ma said. "I can't help thinking there might be more Indians near."

"Shep's watching and I have the rifle loaded and right under my hand," Nathan tried to sound matter-of-fact. "Belle would fight before she'd let anything hurt her foal. The animals would warn us."

"You and your animals," Ma sighed. "let's try and sleep."

—≫ CHAPTER 11 ≪—

fter Pa left the days and nights all ran together. Nathan lost count of everything except the trees he had cut and trimmed. Ma had marked off the days in her almanac ever since she left Kentucky. She said it was Sunday morning, Pa had been gone six days and Nathan should have a rest from his chopping.

"Why don't we go fishing and blackberrying," Betsy asked, "and have another picnic? I'm tired of jerky and cornpone all the time when we could have fish and berries."

"Why don't we?" Nathan said quickly. "There must be lots of ripe berries by now and fish would sure taste good."

Ma took a bite of pone and looked thoughtful. "I don't know whether it would be safe for us all to leave."

"I can take the rifle and we can leave Shep to guard things. We could hear him bark. Ma, the Indians must have gone on or we would have seen them again."

"Let's go fishing," Andy chimed in.

"All right, we'll go," Ma said her face lighting up, "but as soon as we pick the berries and catch a mess of fish, we'll come home."

They were soon ready. There was a well-traveled path now for the horses and Molly followed it as they went out to forage in the morning and came back in the evening.

Shep whined when they left without him, but Nathan knew he would guard the shed and never leave. They had not gone far until Belle whinnied and came to join them, Trinket tagging along behind.

They did not stop at the first blackberry patch, but went on to the second bend in the creek where they had been before. There was bluestem grass in the open place and Belle started grazing.

"I'll pick berries while you children fish," Ma said when they reached the pool. "We can have berries with our dinner. The other patch we'll save for supper like we did before."

Nathan had just put his hook in the water when Ma came hurrying back. "We must go home, right now. The Indians have picked the berries. Not a ripe one!"

"Ah, Ma, how do you know it's Indians?" Betsy moaned as she pulled her first fish from the water.

"Maybe its another settler," Nathan said, "or maybe it's birds or bears!"

"Bears!" Betsy stared at Nathan. Nathan handed his pole to Ma. "You and Betsy fish until you get a mess and I'll keep watch. Everything is all right or Belle would be uneasy." He picked up his rifle and sat down on a stump. Trinket came to him and nudged his arm for petting. "You're a Jim Doosey," Nathan said, "walking clear up here." He rubbed the foal's back and gave her fat little rump a slap.

Nathan watched, but everything seemed serene. White clouds floated in a blue sky and a little breeze stirred the leaves. A bobwhite called from a thicket. He'd be glad when Pa got back and the house was built. He wondered if Walkfast would be here all summer. It felt good to sit on a stump and just do nothing but ponder.

Even Andy caught a fish. When they had fifteen, Ma said it was time to go. Nathan led the way, Trinket followed. They stopped at the second blackberry patch, but it, too, was picked clean. "Whoever picked them might have left one patch," Nathan grumbled. "No need to be so greedy."

Ma was quiet and kept Andy close beside her, Betsy following. Nathan quickened his pace. As he turned the last curve and came in sight of the old camp, he stopped short. Walkfast was sitting on a log looking at them. A bark basket of freshly picked blackberries beside him.

"Walkfast pick berries to eat with the fish and bread," he said as he got up and walked ahead of Nathan to the shed. Shep met them, hair raised, growling at Walkfast, but Nathan quieted him.

There was enough cold pone for the meal and Ma fried the fish just right. Everyone had two big bowls of berries and milk to pour over them. Nathan even poured some milk on a chunk of pone for Shep. Ma thanked Walkfast for the berries and everyone seemed at peace.

Not long after the meal, Walkfast looked around the group, then at Nathan. "I go."

"Come back," Nathan said and smiled at Walkfast. "Sometime when Dick is here, we can see the cave."

Walkfast nodded. "Sometime," he said and without a backward look, disappeared in the direction of Navestown.

"Ma, I never thought you'd invite an Indian to eat with us," Nathan teased.

Ma smiled. "Walkfast is different and he picked all those berries for us. I'm not afraid of him."

"I wonder what Pa will say when we tell him," Betsy said.

"When is Pa coming home?" Andy asked.

"Most any day," Ma replied and smoothed back Andy's hair. "He said two weeks, but knowing your Pa, I think he'll make it sooner."

But at the end of the second week Pa had not come home and Ma kept looking toward the trail to Navestown. Nathan tried not to worry and worked hard chopping logs, but at night he thought about Pa. Where was he? Why didn't he come home? What if he never came back? If something happened to Pa, would they stay here or go back to Kentucky?

The days went by with Ma marking off each one in the almanac, until six weeks had passed. Nathan had cut and trimmed fifty-nine logs and Betsy had burned most of the trimmings. There was a big pile of firewood for Ma to use, and an open space for a garden where the trees had been cut and the sunlight came in. Already Ma had planted some turnips, but it was too late for other things.

The day had been long and hot. Nathan sighed tiredly and mopped the sweat from his face. He had just finished the last tree for the day. Not far away Betsy was piling limbs on the fire and the thick smoke hovered in the still air. Nathan felt as if he had been cutting trees forever. He sat down on a log to rest and Betsy came to sit beside him.

"I'm scared something has happened to Pa, aren't you?" She asked and her voice choked. "He's been gone six weeks. I don't believe he is ever coming back." She wiped her eyes on her sleeve. "Maybe he got the ague and died, or met up with a bear . . . maybe he drowned crossing a river," Betsy looked at her brother.

"I don't think he is dead," Nathan said after a silence. "Maybe he's hurt and not able to travel."

"But what'll we do?" Betsy mopped her eyes and left gray ashes on her face. "Ma gets quieter every day." Her voice fell to a whisper. "You don't think he'd just go away . . . and leave us, do you? Like that man did his family in Kentucky?"

"No!" Nathan spoke sharply, for the same thought had come to him and he felt ashamed. He straightened up. "He's hurt or sick and can't send word. I'm going to keep on chopping logs. Pa says it took seventy-five or eighty for a house. We have to have a place for winter. Pa may come any day, just any day."

But Jesse Nave came instead of Pa, riding in early one morning. He got down from his horse and shook hands all around. Nathan had never been so glad to see anyone.

"I've only been back a week. This time we took the flatboat clear to St. Louis and I thought we'd never get back. I won't do that again."

He cleared his throat. "I hear Mr. Robison left for Lexington to enter the land and hasn't come back yet."

Ma nodded, her face suddenly white. "He planned to be back in two weeks at the most, but it's been nearly two months."

"I may have a bit of news, but not sure," Jesse Nave said and cleared his throat again. "We've asked every stranger that came from that direction for news of Peter Robison. Yesterday some Indian men were in and they told of two men in an empty cabin down by Lexington on the Missouri river. The men had the smallpox and one of them died and the other was alone and barely able to speak. An Indian woman who had had the smallpox went in." Jesse Nave stopped. "I hesitated to tell you," he went on, "for there is no tellin' who they really were and I knew it would upset you, but you should make some plans for the winter. Another six weeks and it will be getting cold."

Nathan looked at Ma, but she did not look up. Her hands were clenched in her lap, the knuckles white.

"Now the Lamson's house is empty," Jesse said, "and I offer you that as long as you need it. I thought you might be willing to have a school there, since you are a teacher. Our younguns need learning. The parents could pay you with provisions and wood for the fire."

"But Nathan's got enough logs for a house!" Betsy cried out.

"You have?" Jesse Nave was amazed. "But it takes at least eighty!"

"I know. Pa said it did. I've been cutting most every day except Sundays and days I had to get meat. I have seventy-six for walls and sixteen extra for the floor. Ma wants a floor."

"Why Nathan! That's most as good as a grown man could do!"

Nathan fiddled with a button on his shirt. "Much obliged," he said huskily.

Jesse Nave rubbed his chin and looked absently across the creek. "Since you've got the logs cut and ready, I think the neighbors should put up the house. After all that work you deserve it. I'll send out the word for the log-raising for a week from today."

"I'll hitch up the mules and drag all the logs up near the site," Nathan promised.

They watched silently as Jesse Nave rode away and disappeared on the trail. Then Ma spoke, "I don't think your Pa was the man that died. He might have been the awful sick one. But I'm not giving up and I don't want you children to. Thoughts are powerful things. Keep thinking and praying that your Pa is coming home."

That night as Nathan lay beside the campfire another thought came to nudge him. He turned it over and over in his mind and tried to push it aside, but it would not go away . . . Shep, knowing something was wrong, curled up beside him trying to comfort him and Nathan finally went to sleep.

—≫ CHAPTER 12 ≪—

It was the day of the log raising. Nathan, Ma and Betsy were up before daylight, but Andy was still asleep in the shed. They had barely finished breakfast when Jesse Nave and two men rode into camp.

"Mornin'" Jesse called. "Brought some good help. Tom Radabaugh and Jim Slaton. Tom's an expert corner man and nobody can rive a clapboard better than Jim. Dick and the women folks are coming soon as they can get things together. Nathan, we're all ready to work. If you'll show us where you want the cabin we'll begin. Brought my whip-saw to use on the floors."

Nathan picked up his axe. "It's right over this way." He walked down the path and the men followed single file on their horses.

"I've staked out the size and the spot," Nathan said. "Pa said the bottom logs should be bigger than the others and I snaked them into place with the mules."

From then on Jesse Nave took over. All morning other men came, some with their families, others alone, some a-foot and some a-horseback. Women brought baskets of food and men brought axes, saws, froes and wedges. Nathan lost count of men and time.

"Having the logs trimmed and cut to a certain length sure cut down on the time," Jesse told Nathan. "And dragging them up here with the mules saved time, too. May get the walls up today, the way things are going."

Nathan tried to help everywhere. Just when, he couldn't remember, Dick was there and other boys came.

At noon someone rang a cowbell and everyone stopped and went back to the shed. Men were handed plates and women passed the victuals.

When the plates were filled, a man Nathan had never seen before held up his hand and the crowd grew still. "Dear Lord, for good neighbors and good victuals, we give thanks. Bless this log-raising and the folks that will live in the cabin and bring their man safe home again. Amen."

Nathan felt sad and lonely hearing the prayer for Pa, ashamed of the thoughts he sometimes had about his father. He saw Ma and Betsy wipe their eyes.

"That was the preacher man from down by Chillicothe," Dick whispered as they started to eat. "He blesses all the log-raisings."

The food tasted extra good to Nathan. There was a huge roast of venison, roasted prairie chickens and smoked turkey. But the roasted prairie chickens tasted best of all. Almost everyone brought fresh Johnny cakes and none of them tasted alike. There were two gallons of wild honey to spread. Ma got out the last of the tea and made a kettle full. It was pale and weak, but everyone bragged how fine it tasted.

Nathan looked around at all the people eating and counted twenty men and twelve women and sixteen children. Some had come from as far as twenty miles. How could he ever repay them? Pa would have to do it . . . if Pa ever came home.

As soon as they had finished eating, the men went back to work. Four men who were expert at notching the logs worked at the corners. After the wall was four logs high, two logs were leaned against the top log and the men rolled the next log up the incline. It was hard, risky work. If a log slipped back, it could break a man's leg or even crush him.

Slowly the walls grew and by night they were ready for the floor of the loft. Some folks from Navestown went back home, but Jesse Nave promised they would be back tomorrow. The others stayed.

After supper the people gathered around the fire and a boy with a French harp played while others sang. Nathan could almost hear Pa's tenor voice leading the familiar song. He tried to sing, but thinking of Pa, the words caught in his throat. If Pa ever came home maybe things would be different. He guessed nobody got to do as they wanted to every time.

Quilts and blankets were spread on the ground and children went to sleep and finally, the fire died down and the night grew still. Belle and Trinket stood for awhile watching from the edge of the clearing, then turned away.

Back in the woods where the strange horses were tethered, came a lonely whinny. Shep growled in his throat and came to Nathan, stretched out on his quilt. Tomorrow, Nathan knew he would be even busier, for Jim Lowe had told him if rocks were brought from the creek and clay from the hill, he would build a fireplace and chimney. Jesse Nave said he was the best chimney man anywhere around.

By sunup the men were working. Nathan and the boys began carrying rocks for the fireplace; two others brought clay. They looped a chain around several big flat rocks to be used for the hearth and the mules dragged them to the site.

Men had sawed a hole in the end of the cabin and built a crib of logs out from it that extended to the roof line. The morning of the third day Jim Lowe began lining the crib with rocks, using clay for mortar. All day Nathan and the boys carried mud for Jim Lowe to put between the rocks, so that when a fire was built in the fireplace it would not set fire to the logs. Gradually it grew into a fireplace inside and a rock and clay chimney outside.

Finally they cut a clapboard roof, pegged it down and the cabin was finished, even to a door that swung on wooden hinges and a wooden latch with a string to lift it up. In a corner someone built a wooden platform about eighteen inches from the floor to be used for a bed.

At noon of the fourth day, the cabin was completed, all

but the chinking with mud between the logs, which Betsy and Ma would try and get done before winter.

When the last peg was driven, Jesse Nave called for everyone to come and they filed into the new room. Ma brought live coals in a pan from the fire before the shed and put them in the new fireplace, then Nathan and Betsy and Andy laid on dry limbs. As the neighbors watched, a little blaze crept up and soon the smoke was drawing up the chimney. Everyone clapped and cheered. "It's good luck when it draws the first time," someone shouted.

Ma turned to the group, her eyes misty. She smoothed back her brown hair and straightened her shoulders. "We can't ever thank you enough for our new home. You've worked so hard and come so far. Peter will . . . thank . . . you too. If we can ever help you, we will."

"She's a brave woman," someone whispered behind Nathan. "Her man won't ever come back. Got only that boy."

"He will come back!" Nathan wanted to shout, but in the dark of his mind, a terrible fear was growing.

The last of the victuals were eaten and the people began to leave. Later the clearing was quiet and seemed lonely after the commotion of the last four days. Several families had brought gifts—a homemade hickory broom, gourds for containers, a hickory basket and cakes of lye soap.

"We will all take a load of things to the new home and get settled," Ma said. "It's surely going to be nice to have a floor again and a door to close at night, even a bed."

"But what's Trinket going to do when she can't sleep by Nathan?" Betsy asked.

Nathan grinned. "I guess I'll have to sleep outside with her."

"She will soon learn to sleep alone," Ma smiled.

Betsy carried Pa's violin and Nathan took the clock box that had never been opened since they left Kentucky. Now Ma unwrapped the old quilt from around the wooden box, untied the leather thong around it and opened the lid and lifted out the Seth Thomas clock her parents had given them when she and Pa had married. There was a tired and lonely look on Ma's face as she set the clock on the mantel. They watched as she opened the glass door and hooked on the pendulum, tied on the weights and wound the clock.

Nathan stepped to the door and squinted up at the sun. "It's about three o'clock," he said. Ma set the hands and started the pendulum swinging. In the stillness the ticking sounded friendly and familiar, like an old friend come to visit. Nathan had always loved the red roses painted on the lower half of the glass door. Grandma used to tell him she grew them in her garden.

"Now if Pa were only here, it would seem like home," Betsy said and her voice quavered. "Ma, you do think he'll come back, don't you? Some of the folks here said he never would and you ought to go and live in Navestown. That it was foolish to build the house."

"Don't you ever believe that," Ma said quickly, but to Nathan her voice sounded anxious and uncertain. The idea Nathan had been mulling over nudged him again as

he went outside to bring the last of the things from the shed.

Ma fixed something to eat and Betsy made a pallet on the new bed and climbed the ladder and spread out Nathan's quilt, too. After supper, Nathan shut the door, pulled the latch string in and climbed the ladder to the loft.

He looked outside through a wide crack. It was bright moonlight and he could see Belle and Trinket waiting for him. He talked to them through the crack and they came to stand beneath his voice.

Downstairs Nathan heard the clock strike as he worried about what he should do. Finally he turned over and with a broken sigh, went to sleep.

In the morning, Ma was up early to milk before she made breakfast in the new fireplace. Nathan went to the creek for a bucket of water. The horses and mules and Molly were round the shed, knowing it was for them now since their people had a house.

Nathan waited until they had finished breakfast before he told them what was on his mind. "Ma, I've been thinking ever since that Indian told about the two men with the smallpox, that I ought to go and see if one of them might really be Pa. I don't feel right to do nothing, now that you've got the house."

"Nathan! What if you didn't come back either?" Betsy cried out, "What if you got smallpox, too?"

"I won't get smallpox. Grandpa vaccinated me, you know that."

"But we don't know for sure if it works," Ma spoke up.

"You've never been exposed since then." She frowned.

"It'll work, Grandpa said so. My arm got real sore, which meant it took, remember? I've thought it all out," Nathan explained. "I'll get a deer so we can make more jerky. I'll tell Jesse Nave where I'm going and maybe Dick can come out now and then to see how you are getting along. When I find Pa, I'll bring him home as soon as he can travel."

"And if you don't find him?" Ma barely said the words.

"I'll go clear on in to Lexington and see if he ever got there. They'll know at the Land Office. Then I'll come home again."

"But Pa said he left you in charge here," Betsy said.

"I know, but Pa's been gone two months. Something is wrong. If I had gone somewhere and didn't come back, Pa would come search for me."

"But you're not a man grown!" Betsy cried out.

Ma kept running her fingers along the hem of her apron like she always did when she was worried. "One of the men said it was wilderness all the way to the Missouri River, and when he went to enter his land, he took off his boots at night and pointed them in the direction he wanted to go the next day so he wouldn't get lost," Ma said.

"How could you ever find which trail Pa took? Nathan, you could get lost." Betsy wiped her eyes.

"I can't find Pa if I don't go and he may be awful sick, or maybe broke a leg," Nathan said gravely. "If you run out of victuals, Betsy, you can go on Spot to Navestown. Jesse Nave will help out."

"Can I go too?" Andy asked, leaning against Nathan.

Nathan looked at Andy and put his arm around his shoulder. "It's too long a trip," he told his brother.

"But I came all the way from Kentucky," Andy said proudly. They smiled at that and Nathan smoothed his hair.

Finally Ma wiped her eyes with her apron and looked at Nathan. "If you think it's best, you go, Nathan. Pa said for you to stay here and look after us, but I give you my word to go. We've the new cabin and I'll feel safe. I'll make more cornpone for you to take along. We can catch some fish . . ."

"Then I'll plan on going early in the morning," Nathan said quietly.

—⇒ CHAPTER 13 ⇐—

When Nathan awakened, it was coming daylight. Down below he could hear Ma moving around. He threw back his quilt and slipped into the clean clothes Ma had given him the night before. Ma was getting breakfast. She looked tired and pale as if she had not slept.

"Are you still of a mind about going?" she asked him.

Nathan was surprised. "Yes, Ma. I thought we agreed on it."

Ma gave a deep sigh and leaned over to stir hominy in the skillet. "We did agree, but I got to worrying in the night, seems things always look worse then. You must be extra careful, Son." She looked up at him and tried to smile. "When you get a bucket of water, breakfast will be ready. I'll wake Betsy. Looks like it will be a nice day."

Outside Shep jumped up and licked his hand and Belle

and Trinket came toward him. "Belle, I wish I could take you, but you'll have to look after Trinket." He petted them both. They followed him to the creek where he got the water, washed his face and slicked back his hair.

Now that he had made up his mind, Nathan was anxious to get on the way. Right after breakfast he saddled Sam and tied on two blankets, one containing a change of clothes for Pa, clean rags and a cake of lye soap, wrapped in a square of oilcloth to be used as a raincoat or windbreaker. In an oilcloth bag Ma put a small kettle, a tin cup and fork and spoon, cornpone and jerky and a packet of salt. It pulled with a drawstring and Nathan hooked it over the saddle horn, along with the picket rope.

The little medicine box Grandpa had given him, Nathan put in an inside pocket. It had quinine, a tin of salve, pills for laxative, a needle and white silk thread for sewing up cuts. A small bottle of laudanum, a package of court plaster and a lump of sulphur. He slipped the powder horn over his shoulder, tied his shot pouch to his belt, picked up his gun and was ready to go.

"Ma, I'll try and send you word with someone coming this way if I have to stay longer than I think. I'll come back as soon as I find Pa, unless he's too sick to ride. Don't you fret. I'll come back."

"I know you will." Ma kissed Nathan's cheek and tried to smile.

Betsy flung her arms around her brother's neck and kissed him, too. "I'm going to stuff cracks all the time you're gone." She choked back a sob.

"I'll tell Jesse Nave I'm going," Nathan promised as he climbed on Sam. "Goodby! Goodby!" He waved and turned Sam toward Navestown, a heavy, lonely feeling in his heart.

Since people came to the log-raising the trail was much better into Navestown. Sam stepped right along. Jesse Nave was walking to his store when he saw Nathan.

"Well, where are you headed so early in the morning?"

"I'm going to try and find Pa. I told Ma that I'd leave word here so you would know, then if they needed help to come in and tell you. After what the Indians told you about the two men in the cabin, I felt sure one was Pa. I made up my mind to go and Ma said I could."

Jesse Nave stared at Nathan. "You're crazy as a loon! Your mother shouldn't have said you could go! If they had smallpox, you'll get it and maybe die, or bring it back here. We sure don't want that!"

"I won't bring it back. One winter when I stayed with Grandpa he vaccinated me and it took. So I can't get small-pox now."

"I've heard of that, but nobody knows for sure. Have you ever been exposed since then?"

"No, but Grandpa's medical book said some people in Boston were vaccinated twenty-five years ago and they didn't get smallpox afterwards when they were exposed."

"Maybe it wasn't smallpox they had. Maybe it was chicken pox," Jesse Nave said shortly. "We don't want smallpox here and that's for sure!"

"I won't bring it back. I promise. If Pa was one of the

men in the cabin, I'll wash his clothes and him, too. He couldn't give it to anybody now. It's been too long. The book said so."

"The book! Maybe the man that wrote the book didn't know smallpox from a hole in the ground!" Jesse said heatedly. "I wish you wouldn't go. If it was Dick and me I'd expect him to stay here with his Ma, like your Pa told you. You can't do any good now and you may get lost, or get chills and fever and not come back home at all. Then what would your Ma do?"

Nathan took a deep breath. "I'm sorry, Mr. Nave," he said quietly, "but I have to go. It would nag me all the rest of my days if I didn't. If it was turned around, Pa would come looking for me."

"That's different. Folks are supposed to look after their younguns." He frowned at Nathan and was quiet for several moments. "But since you're so determined, I'll tell you what I know. I made the last trip to Lexington about two years ago, went twice, once to enter on the land, then to get the patent.

"There's a good trail from here to the ferry over Grand River, then on into Chillicothe. From Chillicothe you angle a little to the east, then south until you come to Jimtown. Only one or two cabins. Don't think the ferry is finished yet. Then you go straight south until you come to a settlement called Carrollton. Maybe forty miles.

"From there keep on south, straight as you can go, until you hit the big Missouri River. All told, forty or fifty miles. At the river turn right and follow it twenty or thirty miles until you come to a ferry, cross over and that's Lexington."

"Where's the cabin the Indians told about?"

"Between Carrollton and Lexington. Some kind of a shortcut. If you ask in Carrollton, somebody can tell you."

Jesse Nave put his hand on Sam's neck and looked up into Nathan's face. "Nathan, the woods are thick and dark on that Missouri River bottom. Be mighty careful. Some characters might take advantage of a boy alone with a good mule.

"There's bears, too, wolves and panthers, so keep your rifle loaded and within reach. I'm warning you, Nathan, what to expect."

"Much obliged, Mr. Nave, for telling me. I'll be careful." He clucked to Sam and turned down the trail. Then Jesse Nave called to him, "Wait, Nathan, wait!" He hurried to the store and came back with a small leather bag of bullets and a horn of powder. "Here take the bullets and let me fill up your powder horn."

Nathan thanked him. "Ma made me some grease squares, now I'll do fine."

A sad look came over Jesse's face as he waved Nathan on. "Good luck, my boy, and a safe journey."

Nathan headed Sam down the trail. As he went out of sight of the cluster of cabins, an empty, gnawing loneliness swept over him. From now on it was an unknown trail. How could he ever find Pa in a dark wilderness where one tree looked like all the million others? He rested the rifle across his shoulder. Once again he was back on the trail, but this time he was all alone.

—≫ CHAPTER 14 ≪—

Nathan looked at the shadows and judged it to be about seven o'clock. Once out of the hills, the trail leveled off across the river bottom and Sam stepped right along. Some of the worry left Nathan and he felt almost happy, for the day was bright and warm. A big buck deer appeared and disappeared like a moving shadow across the trail.

Within an hour, Nathan came to the ferry. A post with a bell swinging from a crossarm also held a lettered sign, *RING BELL FOR FERRY*, and underneath the ferriage rates.

Nathan looked at the river. It was not any wider nor swifter than many streams they had forded coming from Kentucky. He decided to risk it. He guided Sam down to the water and hooked his feet high on the stirrup straps. Sam walked in slowly, the water to his knees, gradually it deepened, coming up to his belly. Nathan stretched up in the stirrups and held the rifle high as Sam swam a few feet, then touched bottom again and clambered up the bank.

The trail from the river led up a long steep hill. At the top was a clearing and a log cabin. A dog ran out and barked and a man came around the house and threw up his hand in greeting. Nathan waved back. The man looked familiar. He called out and Nathan stopped, "Aren't you Nathan Robison where we had the log-raisin'?"

"Yes, I am," Nathan answered.

"Heard anything more from your Pa?"

"No," Nathan replied. "I'm on my way now to see if I can find him."

The man's jaw sagged and he stared at Nathan. "But news got around that he died with smallpox down toward Lexington. Hadn't you folks heard?"

"Yes, Jesse Nave told us that Indians knew of two men in a cabin and they had smallpox. One of them died, but they didn't know if it was Pa. That's why I'm going. I have a feeling one of them might be my father. Anyway, I'm obliged to find out."

"Don't go! If it was that awful disease you'll get it and maybe bring it back to us. What if you die? What'll your Ma do?"

"I won't get it," Nathan said firmly. "I've been vaccinated."

"I don't know what that means, but I do know that only them that's had it can be exposed and not catch it. We don't want no one bringing smallpox around here," he said shortly.

"I won't bring it," Nathan said evenly and started Sam up the trail. No used trying to explain things to folks that don't want to listen or understand, he thought angrily. I'll not use the word vaccination again.

When he came to the settlement of Chillicothe, there was a trading post with a hitching rack in front and at one side a well with a windlass and bucket and a trough for watering horses. Nathan stopped, tied Sam and went inside. A short, stocky man leaned back in a chair tipped against the wall. "Howdy," he said, getting to his feet.

"Howdy," Nathan answered. "I'm on my way to Carrollton and maybe Lexington. Could you tell me which trail to take?"

"Carrollton? Lexington? Seems that's a fer piece for a saplin' like you." The man frowned, looking Nathan up and down. "Where you from? What's your reason for takin' out on your lonesome? Running away?"

Nathan held his temper. "No, I'm not running away," he said levelly. "I'm going to try and find my father. He left home two months ago to enter some land and never came back. I'm Nathan Robison, from north of Navestown."

The man looked at Nathan a moment and his face softened. "Come, I'll show you the way." They went outside and he pointed southeast to a trail that disappeared in the trees. "Stay on that. After a stretch going east, it turns south to Jimtown, about three miles, you'll come to a cabin or two on the banks of Grand River. Cross over and just keep going, mostly straight south except for some jogs and you'll come to Carrollton. Not as big as Chillicothe," he boasted. "From there the road angles off a mite, but mostly you keep going south. Bee-tree hunters were up here last weekend, went back with three wagons loaded with barrels of honey. If they went through Carrollton, the trail should be plain. Been no rain."

"Much obliged for directing me," Nathan said.

As Nathan started to mount, the man stretched out his hand. "I sure hope you find your Pa."

Nathan thanked him and shook hands.

It was only a few miles until he came to a new cabin with a clearing around it. A sign over the door read—CITY OF JAMESTOWN. A woman carrying a baby came to the door when Nathan rode up.

"Howdy," Nathan said. "Is there a ferry crossing here?"

"No, not yet, but my man is going to cut trees to make one. He thinks he'll have it done in a month or so. It's not a very good place to ford the river, but folks do cross. Where are you going?"

"To Carrollton," Nathan answered.

"It's quite a piece down the road, I guess," she said and Nathan felt she had never heard of it. He thanked her and followed the trail to the river. The stream was wider and looked deeper than the east fork. Wagon tracks veered off to the right, but horse and cattle tracks went down the slope into the water. Across the river the south bank had a sandbar and he could see where the tracks came from the water onto the bar.

"Well, if other animals went across I know you can," Nathan told Sam. He held the rifle high up over his head and put his feet up in the stirrup straps again and told Sam to go.

The mule picked his way gingerly down the trail and

stepped into the water. The current was strong and in a few steps Sam was swimming. Nathan stood up in the stirrups, but the water surged up to his waist. Sam was rapidly drifting downstream with the current. Nathan grabbed the bridle rein and pulled hard to the right.

"Sam!" he yelled, "get out of here!" He could feel the muscles of the mule knot with an extra effort and little by little Sam got near the sandbar. Suddenly there was bottom under the mule's feet and he waded up on the bar.

Nathan let down his feet and rested the rifle on the saddlehorn. The mule stood for a minute spraddle-legged and gave a long shuddering breath.

"What a place for a crossing," Nathan muttered as he got down on the sandbar. He walked out of sight of the cabin and took off his boots and clothes. "Soaked to the skin the first day out," he mumbled as he took his bandana from his breeches pocket and wrung it out and began drying his body.

He wrung out his clothes, shook out the wrinkles and spread them on the hot sand, then drained his boots and put them in the sun. The blankets in the oilcloth were still dry.

Nathan hunted a spot of shade. It was almost noon. "Might as well eat while we dry out," he told Sam. The cornpone and jerky tasted good. He would try to make the victuals last until he got to Carrollton.

It was over an hour by the time they were on the trail again. "We have to get halfway to Carrollton before we camp and we've already wasted time by that old river," Nathan complained to Sam.

The river bottom land was flat for several miles before they came to a bluff and rougher country. Hickory and walnut trees were thick among the white oaks and maple. He saw persimmon trees and pawpaw, but the fruit was not ripe. Sometimes there was a patch of open country with prairie grass above Sam's knees. He stopped only once at a little creek to let Sam drink. Most of the trail wound through thick timber. He thought they must surely be halfway when they came to a fork in the trail. Shadows were long and Nathan knew it must be close to sundown. He slouched in the saddle. Neither one of the trails went south. He was tired and had not seen one person since he had left Jimtown.

Overhead doves cooed mournfully and far away he heard a whippoorwill. He got down stiffly from the saddle and walked back from the trail and chose a huge tree with thick leaves. It was soft underneath from years of fallen leaves.

"We'll stay here and decide which way to go tomorrow," he told Sam as he staked him out to graze.

He ate some of the jerky and pone and spread out his blanket, took off his boots and stretched out, his loaded rifle beside him.

Dark came early in the deep woods. He saw a star glinting through the branches and thought of Ma and Betsy and Andy alone in the new cabin. He pulled up the blanket as a mosquito buzzed around him. Jesse Nave had been right. He was a fool for thinking he could ever find Pa in this wilderness.

—≫ CHAPTER 15 ≪—

Nathan slept fitfully. Once he awakened with a start, two red eyes were staring at him from the darkness. He rested his hand on the cold steel of his rifle, lying perfectly still, barely breathing. The eyes went away with a soft padding of feet. Back in the woods he heard Sam snort and knew something was on the prowl. After a troubled sleep he awoke to the soft patter of raindrops falling on the thick tree leaves. Sam was standing under the tree, not far from him, head hanging, sound asleep.

It was barely daylight. Nathan stirred stiffly. He felt he would break if he dared bend. Finally he pulled on his boots, tight and stiff from yesterday's wetting. He reached in the grub sack and got a strip of jerky to chew on as he saddled and bridled Sam. He tied on the blanket and slipped the oilcloth cape over his head. "First creek we'll stop for a drink, unless it rains so hard we can just open our mouths," Nathan said glumly. He led Sam out to the trail where it divided. There were fresh deer tracks going to the left. "Deer wouldn't be going to Carrollton," Nathan mumbled. "We'll try this way." He mounted Sam and turned to the right.

The rain increased until it was a downpour. It dripped off the bill of Nathan's cap and ran down his neck in the back but the oilcloth square kept him dry to his knees. The trail made several curves and once they came to a small lake with wild ducks and geese feeding in it. A cold wind blew in from the water and Nathan's feet were numb and cold in his wet boots. He was hungry. An uneasy fear settled over him. The farther they went, the more he felt he had taken the wrong turn miles back where the trail forked. "We'll go back and start over," he told Sam and turned around. The mule walked a little faster and Nathan knew he thought they were going back to Navestown. He untied the grub bag and took out another strip of jerky and chewed as Sam plodded along.

Hours later they came to the forks of the road. It would soon be too dark to follow a strange trail and Nathan decided to make camp under the tree where he had slept the night before. "A whole day lost," he muttered as he unsaddled Sam and staked him out. Then he ate a bite and rolled up in his blanket with the oilcloth over him, the rifle close beside him.

It was cold and damp and the rain kept on. Finally Nathan went to sleep. He awoke before daylight, so cold and stiff he could hardly move. Sometime in the night the rain had stopped, but the leaves still dripped.

At the fork of the road, they took the left turn, which went southwest, but after a mile or so, it turned back and went directly south. A cold wind came up and Nathan hunched over in the saddle.

It was nearly noon when they came to a clearing with a log cabin. Several dogs ran out and barked. The door opened and two small children looked at Nathan, an older girl watched from behind them. Nathan got off, tied Sam to a post and walked to the house. A woman appeared.

"Please, could you tell me if this is the road to Carrollton?" Nathan asked.

"Yes it is. It's about half a day's journey that-away." She pointed south. "Jest keep on the way you're agoin'. Have you come a fer piece?"

"From north of Navestown."

She shook her head. "Never heered tell of that place."

"It's northwest of the Chillicothe settlement."

She nodded her head. "Heered o' that."

"Much obliged for the directions," Nathan said and turned away. He was almost back to Sam when the woman called out.

"You look kinda tuckered. Would you like to stop and have a bite, such as it is?"

Nathan turned quickly. "I sure would! Even some hot water would taste good."

The woman laughed and the children giggled. The cabin was not clean, but it was warm. A kettle steamed over the fire; the smells of game cooking made Nathan's stomach groan.

The woman dished up a plateful of stew from the kettle, added a chunk of cornbread and, best of all, a cup of steaming chicory.

While he ate, he told the woman his errand to Carrollton, but she did not remember seeing a man on a blaze-faced horse.

Over in the corner, a boy of nine or ten was lying on a pallet. "Is the boy sick?" Nathan asked.

"Johnny's always ailin'," the woman complained. "If it ain't one thing, it's another. He ain't never been strong like the other younguns. Last week he skinned his ankle and now it's festered. Jest won't seem to heal."

Nathan went over to Johnny. "My Grandpa is a doctor and I used to go with him to see his patients," Nathan said to the boy, "Mind if I look at your leg?"

"Of course he don't mind," the mother said and lifted the cover. It was an angry looking wound, the ankle swollen hard and purplish.

"What have you done for it?" Nathan asked.

"There ain't much you can do for a cut except wash it off and let it get well. We're clean out of salve."

Nathan felt a deep anger well up within him. No wonder Johnny was puny. "Do you have some salt?" He sounded like Grandpa.

"Yes, but salt is precious. Got none to waste."

"Do you mind if I try to help him?"

She looked doubtful, then nodded, "Bein' your Grandpa is a doctor."

"Then let's have some warm water in a bucket and a handful of salt."

The girl, Hester, hurried to get a tin bucket half full of water. Nathan dumped in a handful of salt. Then he and the girl helped the boy to a stool. "Put your foot in the bucket and a little at a time, I'll add hot water until it is as hot as you can stand it. It will feel good." He dipped a tin cup into the kettle of water over the fire and carefully poured it in the bucket until the boy shook his head. So far the boy had not spoken and Nathan wondered if he could talk. As the water cooled, Nathan added more until the bucket was two-thirds full. The woman watched for awhile, then turned to the kettle of stew and dished out victuals for herself and the others with a helping on a plate for Johnny. He looked at it sickly and shook his head.

"Some cool water?" Nathan asked, and the boy nodded his head.

The woman spoke up. "Cold water ain't good for him when he's hot as Johnny."

"It will help the fever," Nathan said firmly, "and if he could put his hands in it, that would help, too."

The woman flushed and made no move to get the water, but Hester slipped away and brought back a cup of water. Johnny drank thirstily.

"A pan?" Nathan asked. The girl looked at her mother, then brought a wash basin and handed it to Nathan. "Put your hands in the pan, palm up," Nathan directed, and when he did, Nathan poured a slow stream of cool water on his wrists. Then he emptied the pan into the cup and repeated it several times.

"I can do that," Hester said and took the pan. Nathan kept the water hot in the bucket and Hester poured cool water over Johnny's wrists. Suddenly, Johnny slumped over, and Nathan caught him. The woman cried out, but Johnny slowly straightened up.

"I dozed off," he said weakly, and grinned at Nathan.

"Let's see your ankle," Nathan said and helped Johnny lift his foot. It seemed not quite so red and swollen.

Nathan turned to Hester. "Heat up the salt water and soak his foot three or four times a day, then keep a clean cloth around it between times. Stew some meat and give him the broth. Grandpa says that is good medicine for sick folks."

"Thanks a heap for what you've done. I don't know much about doctorin'. Seems some folks have a knack for it," the woman said. "Stop by again on your way home and I do hope you find your pa."

Nathan thanked her and looked over at Johnny. He was back on the pallet and sound asleep.

Hester walked across the yard with Nathan. As he climbed into the saddle, she looked up at him and said, "Johnny and me are stepchildren. Our real Ma died. I couldn't stand it if anything happened to Johnny." Her chin quivered. "I'm so much obliged for your help."

"I wanted to help. I had to help!" Nathan said almost fiercely. "Some day I want to be a real doctor!"

Hester smiled up at him. "I think you're one right now."

Nathan smiled at her. "Goodbye," he said as he started Sam up the trail.

It must be after two, Nathan judged, but he didn't mind losing the time. He felt very good about Johnny.

It had cleared and the air was crisp. The trail was muddy and in several places Sam had to wade knee-deep where streams of water cut across the trail. The trees seemed ever larger and thicker, and some of the hills were steep. Shadows were getting dense when Sam threw up his head and gave a loud bray. A horse answered him up ahead.

A man on a gray horse came in sight and stopped when he met Nathan. He was lean and tall with dark eyes and jutting chin. "Howdy!" he said in a friendly voice. "What are ye doin' here by your lonesome this time of day?"

"I'm on my way to Carrollton. Could you tell me how much farther it is?"

"About four or five miles, I reckon. One creek out of banks about a mile down the road, but not far across. Your mule a good swimmer?"

"Yes, and much obliged. I want to make Carrollton before night."

"You'll have to hurry. Gettin' dark now."

Nathan thanked him again and hurried Sam down the road. It would have been nice to talk awhile, for this was the lonesome time of the day. He thought of Ma and Betsy and Andy in front of the fire in the new house.

Soon they came to the flooded creek. Sam waded in and for a distance the water was shallow; then suddenly, there was a swift boiling current and Sam was swimming. Nathan held the rifle high and lifted his feet. After a few steps, Sam was clambering up on higher ground where he could wade again.

When it was dark, Nathan loosened the reins and let Sam find his way. Surely Carrollton was not far ahead.

Sam plodded along and when Nathan had almost decided to stop and make a camp, a faint glimmer of light appeared ahead.

The light was in a cabin on the bluff. Dogs ran out and barked. Nathan straightened up in the saddle.

A door opened and a man stood in the light and called out, "Who's there?"

"Nathan Robison from Navestown. Is this Carrollton?"

"This be Carrollton."

Nathan got down and walked stiffly to the door.

"I'm on my way to Lexington. Is there a place where me and my mule could stop for the night?"

"Right here, if you don't mind puttin' your blanket on the floor. At least it's dry and warm and there's some victuals left from supper."

"That's fine for me. And the mule?"

"I've got a corral. Nothin' in there but the cow."

"Is there anything to eat there?"

"Nope."

"Then could I stake him out?'

"Sure can."

With Sam watered and tied out, Nathan and the man went into the cabin. "My name's Pete Johnson and I batch by myself. Got a family back in Indiana. Boy a little older than you. He's bringing them out in the spring."

He cut off a thick slab of venison from a roast and put it on a plate. "Set yourself down to the table and eat." He slid a pan of cornbread before Nathan and set down a bowl of wild honey. Then he sat down across from Nathan. "Now, how about you?"

Between bites of venison and cornbread, Nathan told his story about the Indians and the two sick men in the cabin.

Pete Johnson leaned back and looked at Nathan, dark eyes thoughtful. He smoothed his beard and stared into space for a moment. Nathan felt that Pete Johnson knew something and was deciding what to say. He could feel his heart pounding in the stillness.

"That cabin is an old shack," Pete said at last. "Some say its haunted. Indians go back there to hunt and fish in the lake. They brought the word to the trading post that a white man died in the cabin and they buried him. Said another came and he was awful sick and going to die, too. Thought it might be smallpox. The Indians broke camp. Nobody wants to fool with that disease." Pete Johnson stared into the fire, his face grim. Nathan could not speak.

"No way to tell if one of the men was your Pa, but the signs all point to it," Pete went on. "That news was two or three weeks ago, so your Pa would be dead, or home again long before now. You'll have to face it, Sonny, chances are you'll never see your Pa again."

Nathan felt lost and heartsick. The words sounded cold and final. Pete seemed to know. He made one last try. "Did anybody see a bay gelding with a black mane and tail, a white blaze on his face and four white socks?"

"No. Nobody said anything about seein' such a horse."

"I think I'll turn in," Nathan finally said. "Maybe in the morning I'll know what to do." He spread his blanket on the floor, took off his boots and turned them to the fire to dry out then laid his damp socks beside them.

Pete Johnson put the venison in a tin box and blew out the candle and settled into a bunk across the room. The flame from the fire died down, but tired as he was, Nathan could not go to sleep. Pa had surely been one of the men in the cabin and Pete thought they both died. But Grandpa said not to take things on hearsay, make up your own mind.

He watched the shadows flicker on the wall and turned his thoughts over and over. If Pa had died, was he going or coming from Lexington? Had he been to the Land Office? What about the gold Pa had with him to pay for the land?

Finally Nathan knew what he must do. With a tired sigh he went to sleep.

—⧈ CHAPTER 16 ⧈—

athan awoke to the smell of meat cooking. Steam rose from a kettle on the crane. An iron spider rested on the coals.

"Got the grub all ready, warmed up some roast and fried some mush. It'll stick to your ribs," Pete Johnson said as he put mush and roast on a plate. "Made up your mind about what to do?" He asked Nathan.

"I've decided to go on to Lexington and see if Pa ever entered the land."

Pete nodded. "Good idea."

Nathan hurried through breakfast, saddled Sam, and was soon ready. Pete gave him a chunk of roast to put in his grub sack. "Much obliged for everything," he told Pete. "Felt good to sleep under a roof and dry out."

"You're welcome and if you come back this way, stop again. I'll be wonderin' how you make out."

The sun was up and the sky clear. Smoke drifted up from the other chimneys. One cabin larger than the others had a TRADING POST sign, but Nathan did not stop. Pete had said to keep going south until he hit the river, then to follow along to the right until he came to the ferry. Cross over and that was Lexington.

"Could be thirty or forty miles, don't rightly know," Pete had said.

Nathan urged Sam along. "We're going to try and make Lexington by night, or at least get to the ferry," Nathan told the mule.

As they went along Nathan mulled over in his mind all that Pete had told him about the cabin where the man died and whether or not his father had been in it. He felt sure in his heart that his big, strong father, who could do anything, was still alive. But what had happened to Major? Pa had raised him from a colt and loved him as much as his family, Ma said. Why hadn't Major come home if something had happened to Pa? Maybe Major hadn't lived long enough in Missouri to feel at home and had started back to Kentucky. Worst of all he could have been stolen.

They came to a clearing with a cabin, and again dogs ran out barking. Nathan rode up to the door and called out several times. He looked in the one small window at the end, but there was no one in the room. So he went on.

The trail had been flat ever since leaving Carrollton and they had passed by several small lakes. Ducks and geese were feeding in sloughs that led into the lakes. Sam was hungry and would grab at bushes as he went by.

The forenoon was half gone and the slanting beams of sunlight lay across the trail. Nathan watched ahead and gradually the trail seemed to change. Far ahead a shimmering light grew brighter. A chill, uneasy feeling crept over Nathan. He lifted his rifle to his shoulder. Sam threw up his head and quickened his step. Then Nathan knew. It was the reflection of the sun on water. It was the MISSOURI RIVER!

He urged Sam into a jog trot and they came to a clearing and a log cabin. A path led from the cabin to the river before the trail turned right. Deep and muddy, but shining with reflected light, the river, wide and awesome, swirled and flowed in front of Nathan. Sam began cropping a patch of lush grass and Nathan dismounted to stretch his legs. It was good to come out of the dark woods into the sunlight.

Nathan followed the path towards the river bank. At the edge, steps cut in the dirt went down to the water, and a boy was tying a rowboat to a small tree. "Been fishing?" Nathan called out.

The boy looked up and nodded. He picked up a string of fish from the bottom of the boat and came slowly up the steps. At the top he stopped and looked at Nathan, his brown hair curling out from underneath his cap, blue eyes like a patch of sky. He grinned. "Where'd you come from?"

"Well, I started from up north near Navestown and I'm on my way to Lexington."

The boy looked surprised. "There was a man stayed all

night with us last summer from Navestown. Name was Robison. Know him?"

Nathan grabbed the boy's shoulder and shouted. "Know him? He's my Pa!"

"Your Pa? I do tell!" The boy's eyes grew wide.

"Was he going to, or coming from, Lexington?"

"He was going to Lexington to enter some land. Said he had the best place in north Missouri. Told us all about you'ins comin' from Kentucky. Said they named the new place Poosey, 'cause it seemed like your old home. Said his boy was cutting trees to build a cabin when he got back."

Nathan looked sadly into the boy's blue eyes. "Pa didn't get back. I've come to see if I can find him."

"Didn't get back?" The boy stared at Nathan. "But that was a long time ago."

Nathan nodded. "Been over two months and he planned to be back in ten days or two weeks." He told the boy everything.

"Makes it terrible hard to happen so soon after coming to the new country, doesn't it? Don't know what we would have done if it had happened to us. My name's Len Gaines. Me and Pa and Ma and Goldie live up there in the cabin. We came from Tennessee two years ago."

For a moment they stood quietly. Then Nathan squared his shoulders. "I'll be going along. Helps to know Pa got this far."

"Wish I could tell you more, but I feel in my bones you'll find your Pa. If you come back this-away, stop by."

"I will," Nathan promised as he mounted Sam and

turned toward Lexington. Once he looked back and Len was still watching. Nathan threw up his hand and waved and Len waved back.

The trail followed along the river, most of the way in sight of the water. There were patches of prairie grass, then huge, tall trees arching high overhead. Nathan took out the chunk of roast Pete Johnson had given him and with a piece of cornpone made his dinner. It was the last of the pone. Only a little of the jerky was left. Len had said it was about three hours to the ferry and according to the sun he would soon be there.

The closer they got to the ferry, the more worried Nathan felt. What if Pa had never been to the Land Office? All the old questions and a few new ones came to bother him. Where would he stay tonight? Lexington was a big place. Ma had given him a little money; he would probably have to spend it for a place to sleep.

Gradually the trail widened and led to a clearing. This was the ferry landing with a lettered list of ferriage rates on a painted signboard. A slanting road led down to the water with two solid posts on either side for tying the ferry when it landed. A boy, younger than Nathan, leaned against one post. He looked at Nathan when he rode up.

"If you're wanting to ride the ferry," the boy volunteered, "it's coming across right now. Then Pa goes back."

"Guess I got here just in time," Nathan answered, and the boy nodded.

Nathan dismounted and watched as the ferry came to the landing. It carried a covered wagon with four oxen hitched to it. A woman and children huddled on the seat. A boy about Nathan's age stood beside the rear oxen and a man stood by the lead team. When the ferry reached the bank, a man let the apron down until the heavy planks rested on the bank; then he hurried across to the post and looped a chain from the ferry to the post. After he had done the same on the other side, he motioned to the man. "Drive off!" he said loudly and stepped to one side.

The man by the oxen spoke sharply and cracked a whip, "Buck! Tom! Git along!" The boy at the rear slapped the rump of the ox beside him. The frightened animals stepped warily on the sloping ramp, the whip cracked, voices yelled, and the wagon lurched and groaned up onto level ground.

"All aboard! Last trip today!" the man from the ferry shouted, and Nathan led Sam down the ramp onto the ferry. Sam snorted and shied, but followed Nathan. They were the only passengers.

"Where you from?" the man asked Nathan as he paid his fare.

"Navestown up north of Chillicothe, and I'm going to Lexington to the Land Office."

"Aren't you a mite young to be entering land?" the man said kindly.

"I know," Nathan said. "It was my father that came to enter the land two months ago and he didn't come back. I'm trying to find him."

"Huh," and the man looked keenly at Nathan, "I've seen every man that crossed on this ferry in the last two months. What did he look like?"

"Tall with dark curly hair and broad shoulders. He was on a blaze-faced gelding with four white socks."

The man interrupted, "You're tellin' God's truth! I remember that horse. Man came from Kentucky, didn't he? Why he crossed twice! Said he was from up by Grand River."

"That was Pa! Then he did get to the Land Office!"

"Don't know about that, but he got to Lexington." The man rubbed his chin and looked thoughtful. "So he didn't come back. . . . There's a trail, sort of a shortcut that branches off down the road a piece and goes anti-goglin across to Carrollton. Maybe he took that instead of goin' back the long way by the river. I've heard tell that sometimes things happen along that shortcut. Not good things . . . thievin' and even worse. Maybe your Pa was hurryin' like, took that trail and got waylaid."

"We heard that some men in a cabin got smallpox and one of them died. Ma and I thought maybe one of them was Pa."

"Smallpox!" The man frowned. "Yes, I did hear rumors about that."

"But I don't think Pa was one of the men. I just don't," he said tiredly.

"Well, Son, I'm afraid you're on a wild goose chase. If you've a mind to, though, you can stay the night with us. I'm Bill Jacks. I own the ferry and sometimes we keep folks that get stranded. The Missus always seems to find enough to eat and you can bed down on the floor."

"I'd sure be much obliged. And the mule?"

"He can go in the corral or be staked out."

"I'll stay," Nathan said gratefully.

The boy had been unwinding the chain around one of the posts. Now Bill Jacks unwound the other one and pulled up the apron, securing it to the ferry. Then they were off.

The river wasn't as wide as it had been at St. Louis. Nathan held on to Sam's bridle reins watching as the water flowed past them. It was a well built ferry with rails around the sides. Nathan felt safe as Mr. Jacks guided it with a long sweep from the rear, the boy standing beside him.

After they had tied up on the Lexington side, they walked up to a log cabin, the boy running ahead.

"This is my home," Bill Jacks said, "and you're welcome. Unsaddle and we'll stake the mule out back."

They took care of Sam and went into the cabin. The woman was slender like Ma; her cabin clean, smelling of herbs and spice with game cooking. Cornpone baked by the fire and a baby slept in a cradle. The table was set, with a candle in the center.

"Elmirey, this here is Nathan Robison. He is on his way to Lexington, hunting his father, and I told him he could have a bite with us and stay the night."

She smiled at Nathan, her dark eyes warm and friendly. "There is plenty, such as it is," she said quietly. "I'll put on another plate."

After they had eaten, Nathan told his story once again, and he caught a look between the man and woman when he had finished that told him they thought his father was dead. Everybody seemed to think that. Nathan's throat was suddenly stiff and he could not swallow. For the first time, he began to have doubts about Pa.

"You seem all beat out," the man said as they got up from the table. "Spread your blanket down by the hearth whenever you want to. If sometime in the night someone should bang on the door shouting 'Ferry! Ferry!', pay no heed. They'll just have to wait until morning. Not good for folks to be in such a hurry."

There was another room, and the Jacks and their baby slept there, the boy in the loft.

Nathan took off his boots and stretched out on his blanket, his rifle nearby. He looked at the bundle containing clean clothes for Pa and the little box of medicine and soap. Dully, he wondered if he would ever need any of the things. He watched the fire make threatening shadows on the wall. Tomorrow, he would go to the Land Office.

—≫ CHAPTER 17 ≪—

It was a sunny morning. It seemed about a mile to Nathan before he reached the town. Sam pricked up his ears when he came to the top of the last hill. Sounds of cattle bawling, people talking and wagons squeaking sent a shiver of excitement over Nathan. When he came to the town square it seemed bigger than St. Louis! He pulled Sam over to the side and stopped. Three spans of oxen were pulling a loaded covered wagon. On the side of the canvas were the painted letters, *HEADED FOR SANTA FE*. Behind it came another headed for Santa Fe. Homesteaders' wagons were moving here and there, or pulled over to the side waiting. Saddle horses stood at the hitchrack.

On the sidewalks, men and a few women were bustling along, or gathered in groups talking. Nathan felt a sudden worry about finding the Land Office, but Pa always asked, so Nathan tied Sam and went up to a friendly looking man. "Sir, could you please tell me where I'll find the Land Office?"

The man turned and pointed to a log building. "There she is, plain as the nose on your face. See the sign? Says FEDERAL LAND OFFICE, Rev. Finus Ewing, Commissioner." He looked at Nathan. "Bub, you're too young to try and buy land. Got to be twenty-one, didn't you know that?"

"Yes, I know and much obliged," Nathan answered. He rode over to the building and tied Sam to the hitch-rack. The door was open so Nathan stepped into the small room.

A heavy-set man stood at one end, behind a long table. He was pointing at a crude map on the wall behind him. Two men sat at the table with papers spread out before them. Nathan knew the one standing was the preacher, for he wore a dark coat with his white shirt and tie, his hair combed smooth. He turned and looked at Nathan, smiled and nodded. "Have a chair, Son."

Nathan leaned his rifle against the wall and sat down. The men were entering some land up by Carrollton. They had come from Tennessee in the spring. One of them could not write. Finally they were finished and the preacher folded up the papers. "I'll see that these go out by the next stagecoach. Come back in two or three months. We may have word by then. Mail has been coming through pretty fast lately. Got some patents yesterday that only took two months."

The men shook hands with the preacher, pleased looks on their faces. They spoke to Nathan as they went out.

The preacher looked at Nathan. I'm Finus Ewing," he said and put out his hand as Nathan came to the table. "What brings you here?"

Nathan shook hands and sat down at the table. He cleared his throat and found it hard to speak. "I'm Nathan Robison from up by Navestown, between the forks of Grand River. My father, Peter Robison, left home the last of July to come to Lexington. He . . . never came back. Did . . . he ever enter some land?"

"He sure did, and what's more, the patent came back with some others just yesterday." He pulled out a drawer, shuffled through some thick envelopes, then smiling triumphantly, he came to one and took it from the drawer. "Here it is!" He took out a sheet of parchment that crinkled when he spread it out on the table before Nathan.

"I have the receipt right here," Finus Ewing said opening the book. "Paid to Finus Ewing the 29th day of July, 1837, by Peter Robison, $50 in gold for forty acres of land between the Thompson and Grand Rivers, Livingston County, State of Missouri." Finus Ewing read the exact description of the land, then stood up pointing to a place on the map. "This is the Grand River and this the Thompson river. Some folks call it the east fork of Grand River. Your father's land is right about here."

Nathan leaned across the table thinking of Ma, Betsy and Andy on the land, waiting for him to bring Pa home. He looked down at the patent, his heart thumping as he read the official words signed by Andrew Jackson, President of the United States. Pa really owned the land with the new house on it!

"If you can write, you can sign your Pa's name here in the book and underneath sign your own. This will show I delivered the patent papers to you," Finus Ewing said kindly. "It is a valuable paper and you need to take mighty good care of it until you get back home."

Nathan signed his father's name, then underneath, by Nathan Robison, son, and the date, Sept. 23, 1837.

"There! That makes it official," Finus Ewing said as he folded the crisp thick paper and slipped it back into the envelope. He handed it to Nathan. "Put it in a safe pocket so you won't lose it."

"Now, about your father. Maybe he is still in Lexington waiting for the patent to come. A few have done that so as not to make a second trip."

"Pa said he'd be back sure by two weeks, then we'd build the cabin. He marked the trees I was to cut while he was gone."

The preacher's eyes were kind as he looked at Nathan. "Son, does your Pa partake of the vine?"

"Vine?" Nathan was puzzled.

"Does he drink wine or whiskey?"

Nathan flushed with sudden anger. "No! Pa is restless and doesn't want to live in crowded places, but he is not a tippler. He likes to sing and play the fiddle, but he's no fly-by-night!"

Finus Ewing's kind face reddened slightly. "No need to

get riled. I want to help, but we have to face facts. You say he sings and plays the fiddle?"

"But he didn't bring his fiddle. He intended to hurry right back to get the new house built and get settled before winter." Nathan leaned toward the preacher telling him everything he knew from the time his father left until that minute.

"Let me think," Finus Ewing said and looked absently out of the door. Now and then he would shake his head as if he thought of an idea and rejected it.

"I've heard of this shortcut that angles off from the ferry to Carrollton. Awhile back a traveler left here and went that way and some ne'er-do-wells followed him and waylaid him. Took his money and his horse and set him a-foot. This could have happened to your Pa, or he could have got sick with chills and fever."

He shifted in his chair and looked straight at Nathan. "One thing I do know. You shouldn't get any ideas about taking the shortcut, a boy like you. If your Pa got sick he would have either been gone by this time, or surely be able to get somewhere for help. This is a frontier town, Son. All kinds of people come here from the east and south. Good and bad, Nathan.

"The thing for you to do is go back the way you came and get the patent safely to your mother. Your Pa would want that."

Nathan looked into the preacher's eyes and saw only pity. Finus Ewing was just like everyone else. He, too, thought Pa would never come home.

Nathan had never felt so lost and friendless. He looked at the spot on the map Finus Ewing said was Poosey and tried to think.

Across the table the preacher reached out his hand and bowed his head. Nathan shut his eyes. "Our Father, if Peter Robison is alive, watch over him and bring him safely back to his family," the preacher prayed. "Help this boy on his journey home. Guide every footstep of his mule. Give him courage and strength. Amen." The words seemed to echo in the room and Nathan sat quietly.

The preacher took out a thick silver watch from his vest pocket. "It's nigh dinnertime," he said to Nathan. "Come along home and eat with us. We can put your mule in the barn and feed him, too. He looks kinda gaunt."

"The ferryman's wife gave me something to eat, but if you'd feed Sam I'd be thankful. He's been on short rations ever since we left home."

"Shucks! Save the grub Mrs. Jacks gave you. You and the mule come with me. There's always an extra plate on our table."

Nathan led Sam as they walked down the street. It seemed the preacher knew everyone and called out greetings. They came to a two-story log house a few streets over. "This is our home, serves as a church on Sundays and on Wednesdays for prayer meetings and sometimes in between for weddings. But we go to the river for baptizings."

They watered Sam then tied him in a stall in the barn with several ears of corn in the box and hay in the manager.

"Let me pay for this," Nathan insisted as he took out his purse.

The preacher shook his head. "Take it and be thankful. It was given to me for marrying a couple over a year ago. Their first baby turned out to be twin boys and the father was so happy he brought me an extra load of corn and hay."

The Ewing house seemed full of children. Mrs. Ewing, plump and serene, smiled at Nathan over a steaming dish of hominy she was putting on the table. A girl older than Nathan helped her and two smaller boys pulled up stools and benches. The preacher took his place at the head of the table motioning Nathan to sit beside him. They were all quiet for the blessing, then everybody began talking and laughing.

When the preacher finished eating he shoved back from the table. "I always go right back to the office, might be someone waiting," Finus Ewing said.

The little boy next to Nathan giggled. "He takes a nap," the boy whispered.

Nathan got up to go with him. He thanked Mrs. Ewing, but she was so busy with the baby she only nodded.

"I've been thinking," the preacher said as they went outside. "It might be a good idea to see Doc Maberry. He goes across the river and everywhere around. He might have had some word of your Pa, or even been called to doctor him. I'll show you where he lives."

"I'm so much obliged for the victuals," Nathan said, "and for feeding Sam."

"It's a preacher's business," Mr. Ewing said, "to help folks and their critters."

Nathan got Sam and they walked along the street with Finus Ewing. Nathan decided he liked Lexington. The preacher pointed down the road. "Go down that way until you come to a log house with a big red oak in the yard, turn left and go on until you come to a two-story log house with a split-hickory fence around it. That's Doc's. His office is in the room downstairs on the right. A nameplate on the door says *JAMES MABERRY, M.D.* Just open the door and walk in. Everybody does. Chances are he won't be there, so just set and wait. He'll come back. I'd sure see him before you start home. He might know all about your father. Between the two of us we usually know what's going on."

Nathan thanked him again and turned toward the doctor's home.

—⇒ CHAPTER 18 ⇐—

he doctor's two-story house was big with chimneys on each end and a porch across the front. Several horses and a team were tied to the hitchrack. The shingle beside the door said, *OFFICE OF JAMES MABERRY, M.D.* Nathan opened the outside door and stepped into a wide hall. The door on the right was open. Several people were in the room, a family with children, the mother holding a baby who cried pitifully.

A girl near Nathan's age in a dark dress and white apron came from a back room. Braids of yellow hair wound around her head like a crown. She looked at Nathan, her gray eyes warm and friendly. "Did you want to see the doctor?"

"Yes, but I'm not sick. It's about my father."

"The doctor is out on a call and I don't know when he will be back. He left before daylight. What seems to be the matter with your father?"

"Well, maybe nothing," Nathan stammered, embarrassed. "You see, I don't know where he is. He left home in July to come to Lexington, but he never came back. Mr. Ewing thought Dr. Maberry might know about him or have been called somewhere to doctor him."

"Pa never said. Why don't you just wait. He might know something."

Nathan found an empty chair and sat down. One of the children came over to him wanting to talk. "We've been here ever since morning. Timmy cries all the time. His stummick hurts. Ma says he'll die if Doc can't do something."

"The doctor probably can help him," Nathan said trying to comfort the boy.

"The man over there cut his arm bad. He came right after we did. Will he die, too?" The boy asked.

"No, the doctor will fix his arm and he'll be as good as new." The child looked relieved.

Two boys came in the front door and went up to the girl and held out a bottle. "Miss Annie, Ma said she wanted another bottle of the cough medicine. She thinks it helps."

Miss Annie took the bottle into the adjoining room and brought it back full of red liquid.

"Ma said that Pa will bring you a bushel of turnips, as soon as they grow a mite more."

"That will be fine," Miss Annie said and smiled at the boys. "I'll write it down in the book."

The baby never stopped its sad little moaning. Annie

held him to rest the mother. She tried to give him liquid with a spoon, but he wouldn't swallow. Nathan wished he knew something to do for the baby. He went out into the yard and the man with the cut arm came too.

"Hard listening to a sick baby," the man said. "I wish the doctor would come."

"Yes, I do too," Nathan said. "Does your arm hurt bad?"

"Yes, pretty bad. You see, I was sharpening a fence post when the axe hit a knot and slashed my arm. Miss Annie says it will have to be stitched up and if she says so I believe her. She reads Doc's books and goes with him sometimes on his calls. Some folks think it ain't ladylike, but Doc needs help, ain't got no boys. Five girls." He looked down the road, then back again. "My, I wish Doc would come. I just don't know what Nellie will do if I don't get home by dark. She'll think I've bled to death, or a bear got me."

"He'll surely come soon," Nathan said, trying to encourage the man.

"Too bad about your Pa," the man said, forgetting his own troubles for a moment. "You the oldest?"

Nathan nodded.

"Then it will fall on you to take his place. Your Ma is lucky to have you to make the living. Seems we all got our troubles."

The man went back inside, but Nathan stayed out, standing by Sam, wondering when the doctor would come and if he would know anything about Pa.

It seemed right to be in a doctor's office again, as if he belonged there. He thought of Grandpa wondering if he was out on a call. He sat down on the fence.

Suddenly a loud wailing broke out in the office, not the baby's cry, but a grown person. Nathan got up and hurried to the door. Miss Annie was holding the baby, her ear against its tiny chest listening, Nathan knew, for a heartbeat. Then she handed the limp little body back to the mother. "Your baby's gone, Mrs. Landon. I'm so sorry Pa wasn't here, but I doubt he could have saved it."

The woman cried out again holding the baby close against her breast. The children leaned against her sobbing. Their father wiped his eyes with his sleeve and patted his wife awkwardly. "Let's go, Amelia. Tomorrow we'll get the preacher to bury him by little Randolph."

Miss Annie went out of the room wiping her eyes. The room seemed strangely empty, yet the whimpering cry of the sick baby lingered. Only the man with the cut arm and Nathan were left.

New sounds from the back of the house grew louder. A tall, gaunt man came through the door to the inner room. It was the doctor. He nodded at Nathan and spoke to the man. "Annie tells me you've waited all day with a cut arm. I'm sorry. Come in and we'll take a look."

They went into the inner room and the doctor shut the door. Shortly it opened again. He looked at Nathan. "Could you give me a hand? Annie usually helps but she's upset about the baby dying."

Nathan got up, his mind a blur, his heart thumping.

The man was lying on a narrow table. The doctor strapped his feet down and fastened another across the man's chest. "Just so you won't get up and sock me one right in the middle of things," the doctor said to the man.

The doctor handed Nathan a pair of short tongs with a wad of cotton clamped in the end. "Now, when I begin to take the stitches, mop up the blood so I can see. There's more cotton in the jar when you need it."

He reached into a cupboard for a bottle of whiskey and poured out a glass half full. "This will help cut down the pain."

The man shook his head. "No, I'll just grit my teeth. Might go to sleep on the way home."

The doctor unwrapped the injured arm and threw the soiled rags in a tall can beside the table. Then he washed all around the cut with soap and water. He picked up a white cloth and folded it into a thick little pad. "Open your mouth," he told the man. "As long as you are going to grit your teeth, might as well have this pad to chew on."

The doctor looked at Nathan. "Sure this won't bother you?"

Nathan shook his head. "I've helped my grandfather. He's a doctor."

"Fine!" the doctor said. "We'll talk about that later."

It took fifteen stitches to close the wound. Nathan mopped and watched exactly how the doctor did it. The man groaned, swearing around the pad between his teeth.

"There!" the doctor finally said as he began to bandage the arm. Nathan loosened the straps. "It's all finished.

Come back in a week and we'll take a look. If I'm not here, Annie will know if it's doing all right. If it is, she'll take out the stitches. Here's a couple of opium pills to take when you get home."

The man got off the table, looking white and shaky. He stood for a minute to steady himself.

"Think you can make it all right?" the doctor asked.

The man nodded. "I have to. Nellie will be worried." He walked slowly to the door and left.

"Now what's wrong with you?" the doctor asked as he wiped the needle and put it in a little case.

"Nothing wrong with me," Nathan said. "Mr. Ewing thought I should come here to see if you knew anything about my father. He left home in July and . . . ."

The doctor interrupted. "Have you had your supper?"

"A . . . little . . . jerky . . . from my grub bag," Nathan stammered in surprise.

"Well, I haven't eaten either, so come back to the kitchen and have supper with me, then you can tell your story. We can kill two birds with one stone. I'm bone-tired and half-starved."

They went to the back of the house. It was a different world. A long table with a red checkered cloth sat in front of a row of glass pane windows, a little curtain of the same checkered cloth at the top. The narrow shelf over the window held blue plates set up like pictures. A small pretty woman with hair the same color as Annie's was rocking in a chair, knitting. Annie was looking at a book and put it down when they came in. They looked so strong and healthy to Nathan it was hard to believe they had anything to do with sick folks.

"Nathan Robison, meet my wife, Mary. You already know Annie. The other girls have gone to bed. Could we have a plate for Nathan?"

Annie, Nathan and the doctor sat down at the table and Mary went back to her knitting.

"Now," the doctor said, "let's hear your story."

Nathan told his story. "Pa got here all right and paid his money and the patent came back yesterday. I signed for it and have it in my jacket pocket."

He told about the shortcut and the rumor of smallpox. He mentioned everything that had happened since Pa left, even about Kentucky and wanting to be a doctor. "Mr. Ewing thought maybe Pa had gotten sick and you'd been called to doctor him, or maybe you'd heard some talk. He thought you might know."

The doctor leaned back in his chair and pondered what Nathan had said.

"I wish I did know something, but I don't. I've heard of the shortcut, but never been on it. I heard rumors about the smallpox, too, but I haven't run into any of it. Sometimes people think it is smallpox when it is a bad case of chickenpox." He looked searchingly at Nathan. "Did your grandfather vaccinate you?"

"Yes, and it sure took," Nathan said wryly.

"Did he graduate from Edinburgh?"

"No, but he studied and served under a doctor that did."

"Why do you want to be a doctor?"

"Because . . . because I want to help people get well and live! My mother almost died coming up from Kentucky!"

The doctor nodded his head. "You going to study with your grandfather?"

Nathan hesitated, the old resentment against Pa welling up in his heart. He was surprised the doctor would ask.

"I don't really know. I wanted to stay in Kentucky, but Pa thinks me wanting to be a doctor is just an idea I got from Grandpa. So I had to come with the family to Missouri. Grandpa gave me one of his books to study. I read it when I have time, but I won't be twenty-one for six more years and if Pa wants to keep me that long I have to stay. And . . . if . . . I don't find Pa I'll just have to forget about wanting to be a doctor so I can take his place making a living for the family."

The room was quiet. A log burned through in the fireplace and fell apart sending a shower of sparks up the chimney. The doctor gave a tired sigh straightening up in his chair looking at Nathan.

"If for any reason you might be free to study medicine and decide it is too far back to Kentucky, come study with me. I have all my books and you could use them, then you could go on to medical school when you've learned all I know. But make no mistake, it's a hard road and you're responsible for life and death. But you said you wanted to help people, not just be a doctor to make money, or for standing in the community. That makes all the difference." He smiled for the first time. "You could room and board with us, free for the help you'd give me." He turned to his wife. "Is that right, Mary?

She looked up and smiled at Nathan. "Yes, I'd be glad to have you. Jim needs help so much."

Nathan stammered his thanks, too astonished to think.

"Carry it in your mind. I wish you all the luck in the world in finding your father. Miracles do happen. I've seen some of them. Bring in your blankets and sleep on one of the couches in the waiting room. They aren't bad. I've finished up many a night on one of them."

Annie spoke, "I've been thinking about the patent in your jacket pocket. You could lose it so easy. If you will give it to me, I'll sew a cloth around it, then if you'll take off your shirt I'll sew the cloth to that."

The doctor laughed. "Trust Annie to think of something, but I'll go her one better. Sew the patent to the inside of his undershirt under the left arm, less wear and tear on it there."

Nathan took the patent from his jacket pocket and Annie sewed a piece of white cloth around the envelope, then to the undershirt.

The doctor yawned and said good night. "Come on Mary, let's go to bed. Everyone pray that nobody comes to wake me."

Nathan put on his shirts and picked up his jacket. "I sure do thank you, Miss Annie, for fixing the patent. I can't lose it now." He smiled down in Annie's face. "You got awful pretty hair," he blurted out, then felt his face flush.

"Thank you," Annie said and put her hand on Nathan's arm. "I hope you get to be a doctor. You'd make such a good one."

"I'm much obliged," Nathan said. "I'm sorry about the baby. You did everything you could. Sometime somebody will learn how to save them. I wish I could be the one."

Nathan said goodnight and went out to Sam to get his blanket from behind the saddle. "I'm sorry, Sam, to leave you tied up all night. Anyway, you did have a good feed at noon."

The doctor's prayers were not answered. Sometime in the night, a man knocked on the door and soon after, Nathan heard hoofbeats as the doctor's horse went past the house to the street.

In the morning Nathan had breakfast with the family, and Mrs. Maberry insisted that he put Sam in the barn and feed him. She fixed Nathan some bread and meat to take with him.

"I'm so much obliged for the bed and victuals and most of all for the invitation to come to study and live here. I won't ever forget that." He shook her hand.

He turned to Annie. "And thanks again for sewing the patent in a safe place."

"Maybe some of your neighbors will come to Lexington to enter their land and you can send word about your father. We'd like to know," Annie said earnestly.

Nathan watered Sam, rode out to the street and turned toward the ferry. He looked back. Annie was standing on the front porch waving to him. He waved back, a mixture of joy and sadness in his heart.

—⟫ CHAPTER 19 ⟪—

It was nearly noon when Nathan boarded the ferry. After the apron was secured and William Jacks had started across, he motioned to Nathan. "Well, what did you find out?"

Nathan told him about talking with Finus Ewing and Pa buying the land and the patent arriving. He told about staying at the doctor's, but that the doctor hadn't heard anything about Pa and knew only a rumor about the smallpox. "He'd never been on the shortcut, but I think I will go back that way even though some say it isn't safe. I know Pa isn't on the road I came down. He was probably hurrying to get home and went the short way."

"Don't be a fool and risk your life when your Ma has only you!" Mr. Jacks said gruffly. "You've got the papers, go home the way you came."

"Are there any cabins on the short cut?"

"Two or three I've been told, but I don't rightly know. Never been there."

"Doesn't anyone ever come out from there?" Nathan persisted.

"Indians spend time back there on a lake in the summer. Sometimes somebody from Carrollton cuts through, or a traveler gets lost or somebody gets in a mighty hurry, but it's no place for a boy by himself. You might not see a soul, then again you might. It's damp and swampy and full of ague."

As they landed, Nathan told Mr. Jacks goodby and rode up to the cleared spot to watch the ferry load and start back across the river. Then, with a long, deep sigh, he turned Sam toward the shortcut, his loaded rifle over his shoulder.

The trail was poorly marked. Tall trees met overhead, the shadows were thick and dark. They came to a swampy place where Sam sank to his knees for several steps, Nathan held his breath, fearing quicksand. But Sam struggled onto firm ground and they went on. It was an eerie place. Sam kept flicking his ears, catching every sound.

Hours later they came to a clearing with a log cabin. A thin spiral of smoke rose from the chimney. A big black dog, tied by the door, barked straining at the rope. Without dismounting Nathan called out, "Anybody home?"

The door opened a crack and a thin, white-faced boy opened the door to silence the dog. "Nobody home but

Ma and me and she's sick with the chills," he said without smiling.

"I wanted to ask about a man who might have come this way about two months ago," Nathan explained. "He was my father."

The boy shut the door and Nathan waited, afraid that he would not come back. Maybe Pa was in the cabin?

Nathan sat tensely in the saddle, waiting, listening. Finally the door opened wider and the boy spoke, "Ma says you can come in if you ain't afeared of catchin' the fever."

"I'm not afraid," Nathan said and dismounted. He tied Sam to a tree and went to the door, the rifle in the crook of his arm. The dog growled, but did not try to bite.

The dirty room smelled of hides and fish. A thin woman, her face flushed with fever lay on a crude bed in the corner of the room. Her dark eyes searched Nathan's face.

"Amos says you're lookin' for your Pa that came by late summer."

"Yes. He left home near Navestown over two months ago and came to the Land Office at Lexington. I'm trying to find him. He was tall and square-shouldered with black hair and dark eyes. He rode a bay horse with a white blaze on his face and four white socks, black mane and . . ."

"I remember the horse," the boy interrupted.

"Then he did come by here?" Nathan turned eagerly. "Going northeast?"

"Headed thataway," the boy pointed north.

"Don't many folks go by," the woman said weakly, "so it ain't hard to recollect. I told my man this was an unhealthy place to settle. Some of us have the ague all the time. I been up and down all fall, so I didn't see your Pa. Amos, some water."

The boy got a dipperful of water from a bucket and the woman drank it eagerly, lying back limply on the pallet.

"Have you been to a doctor?" Nathan asked.

"La no! My man did get some quinine in Lexington, but it's all gone. Seems when you get the chills and fever, you just can't get shut of it. Amos had the fever, too."

Nathan thought of the quinine in his little box. He looked at the sick, feverish woman and the listless boy.

"My grandfather is a doctor," he said quietly. "I used to go with him on calls. I have a little quinine I brought along, thinking my Pa might need it. I'll share with you." He reached into his pocket and brought out the little box, unwrapped it and took out the bottle. Amos brought their old empty quinine bottle and Nathan carefully transferred several doses of the white powder on the tip of his knife.

"You're good as a real doctor," the woman said gratefully. "I wish I was well enough to cook you some vittles, but I can't seem to get any strength. Maybe I'll do better with the quinine. I'm so much obliged," she said with tears in her dark eyes.

Amos followed Nathan out and twice the boy started to speak, then stopped. When Nathan was on Sam, he picked up the reins. "Much obliged for the news of Pa and I do hope your mother gets better."

Then Amos leaned close and looked up into Nathan's eyes. "The trail's bad farther on . . . watch out for bad places."

"You mean swampy places and quicksand?"

"Yes, and other things!" The boy said and suddenly stepped back.

"What other things?" Nathan asked, leaning closer to the boy, a chill spreading over him.

"Bear and Indians . . . and . . ." Then the boy turned and would not say more.

Reluctantly Nathan started Sam on the trail, his rifle cradled in his arm, a deep foreboding within him.

Part of the trail was soggy, low-hanging branches and sharp briers swiped against them. There was no sign of cabins. Sam was slowing as he picked his way along the trail. Under a thick canopy of trees it was already twilight. When they came to the shore of a lake, Nathan stopped to rest his legs and let Sam drink. Every bone ached with tiredness. They could not be far from Carrollton and the last chance of finding Pa would be gone.

Long shadows stretched across the still water. Finally, he knew in his heart what all the others had been telling him was true. Pa was gone and he would never see him again. The old sour thoughts nudged him. He remembered the way he had acted like a peevish child because he could not stay in Kentucky. He was sorry, ashamed. He wished he could tell Pa.

Now he would have to go back home with the patent papers and take his father's place. He would have to forget

all about wanting to be a doctor. He'd be too old when Andy was big enough to take over the farm, too old to go back to Kentucky or Dr. Maberry's to study.

As all the bitterness and heartache washed over him, dry hard sobs shook his body and he leaned against Sam letting the grief and disappointment come out. Sam turned his head and lipped the sleeve of Nathan's jacket. Nathan tried to say something to the mule, but no words came. When his storm was over he felt old and empty, washed out, as if he would never talk, or think or laugh again.

He looked dully up the trail. Black shadows lurked under the thick trees. Nathan turned to the openness of the lake and decided to bed down for the night. In the morning he would go on to Carrollton and home.

He staked out Sam and hunted for a dry spot to spread his blanket, eating a small chunk of Johnny cake the doctor's wife had given him.

A thin sickle of a moon shone low in the west. The stars that had seemed so near and friendly now seemed far away. Poosey Ridge, Kentucky was another world and Poosey, north Missouri just a dream. Nathan curled up on the blanket pulling it over his head to keep away the mosquitoes, the loaded gun beside him. Bull frogs croaked along the lake and crickets fiddled in the rushes, but Nathan did not hear them.

The mule browsed in the dark circle and finally came to stand near the boy under the blanket, head down, eyes closed, then he too slept.

—≫ CHAPTER 20 ≪—

The moon set, a soft breeze came up rustling the tree tops and riffling the still water. In the east, the sky lightened. Down by the lake, a horse came from the forest to the edge of the water and leaned over to drink. A strange, yet familiar scent came downwind, the horse lifted its head. It scrambled up the bank and let out a high, ringing neigh that echoed and re-echoed the length of the lake.

The mule stirred, lifted his head, long ears alert as the neigh came again. Then he split the air with a raucous bray that jerked Nathan straight up. He threw back the blanket, his hand on the rifle. For an instant he could not think where he was, then he knew and knelt in the soft earth, the rifle cocked, ready, remembering the things he had been warned about.

Faintly he heard a horse galloping up the trail, hoofbeats coming closer and closer. Sam brayed again, and back came a high, excited whinny. Nathan held steady, but a wild hope raced through his mind and clutched his throat.

Out of the shadows came the horse, the familiar white blaze on his face etched against the darkness.

"Major! Major!" Nathan stumbled up to meet him. "Where'd you come from?"

The horse trotted over to them, his brown eyes wide. He nudged Nathan's arm nickering soft, fluttery sounds of greeting. Sam reached over to nip Major's side and rub his nose against him.

Nathan laid his head against Major's neck and tangled his fingers in the horse's mane. "Major, where's Pa?"

There was no saddle or bridle on the horse. Across one flank and along his side were fresh, red, angry scars. His tail was matted with burrs and his fetlocks and white socks caked with mud.

The horse tramped around nervously. Nathan hurried to loop up the picket rope and fasten his blanket to the saddle. He mounted Sam, his rifle cradled in his arm. "Major, take us to Pa, take us to Pa."

Major was used to leading and he started ahead. Though the sky was light, it was almost dark in the shadowy forest. Major went on as if he knew the way. They followed the trail until they came to a place where a little spring made a deep pool. The trail went on toward Carrollton, but a path branched off to the right and disappeared into the forest. Major turned on it, walking faster as if he had traveled it many times. The path turned to skirt a huge fallen tree and on the other side, in a little clearing was a cabin, the door open. Major went slower and gave a little nicker.

"Pa?" Nathan called out. "It's Nathan!" There was no answer.

He hurried to dismount, a cold chill creeping over him. He was suddenly afraid of what he would find. He called again, waiting for some sound, but none came, only the faint quack of ducks on the lake and a woodpecker drilling high in the top of a dead tree.

Nathan tied Sam and walked slowly to the door. Over in the corner a man lay on a pallet on the dirt floor, his body partly covered by a blanket. His hair was matted, his beard dirty and foul. It couldn't possibly be Pa, for Pa was strong and proud. Nathan went over to the pallet and looked down into the thin, haggard face. He knelt beside the man, unbelieving.

"Pa?" He whispered, choking over the name. "Pa?" He took the thin hand in his own and looked at the fingers. There was the middle one without a tip that Pa had cut off with the hatchet and the long scar across the back of the hand. Nathan remembered how sore the hand had been, how Ma had bandaged it. He touched the wrist hunting for a pulse and found it faint, but steady. A scab on Pa's forehead looked suspicious. Nathan opened the undershirt and looked at Pa's chest. Pock marks were thick upon it. Tears filled Nathan's eyes. How could he have ever felt hateful toward this man?

Something snapped behind Nathan. He whirled to his feet. It was Major standing in the door. Nathan could tell from the dirt floor that the horse had been here many times. There were even hoofprints near the pallet where Major must have stood.

Nathan choked back a cry and squatted beside the wraith of a man. "Pa!" he said and shook his father's shoulder gently. "Pa, it's Nathan. Open your eyes and look at me. I've come to get you well and take you home. Ma's waiting for you. Pa?"

The eyes in the sunken face partly opened, unseeing. "Nathan" the parched lips barely formed the word and the eyes closed again. A flood of love and gratitude rushed over Nathan. Pa knew him! Suddenly there were a dozen things to do.

Nathan took off his jacket and hung it outside on a tree. The sun was up and lighted the little clearing. He broke off dry branches from the fallen tree, and picked a handful of dry grass. Carefully he made a little pyramid in the fireplace, taking the flints from his pocket and striking them together until the spark caught, making a tiny blaze, nursing it along until he had a fire.

Outside, he unwrapped his blanket and took out the rags and soap and the little kettle Ma had insisted he bring along. He ran to the spring and filled the kettle.

"Water," Nathan barely heard the whisper.

"Yes, Pa. Right here." Nathan half-filled the tin cup and, lifting Pa's head, poured a swallow into his mouth. It finally went down, then another and another. "There, that's enough for now." Nathan eased his father's head back on the blanket.

Nathan put a chunk of wood on the fire, picked up his rifle. "I'm going to get us some meat, but I'll come back soon. Major and Sam are here with you. Keep listening for me. "Pa? You hear?"

A faint nod was the answer.

Nathan hurried toward the lake. A duck seemed the quickest if he could sight one near the bank. The trail followed the lakeside and Nathan picked his way carefully along it. When he could hear the ducks quacking and feeding, he slipped over to a thicket beside the lake and peered out. In front of him the water was dotted with mallard ducks, some up· on the bank feeding on weedseed. Maybe if he was lucky he could get two with one shot. Pa had done it.

He parted the bushes and took careful aim, but only one duck fell when he shot. That was enough for now. He did not wait to pick off the feathers, but skinned and dressed it, hurrying back to the cabin. The water was boiling in the little kettle and Nathan cut up the duck and dropped it in. It would soon make broth for Pa.

He unsaddled Sam and staked him out. He hung the saddle and bridle in the cabin. He found some chips by a stump. They would do for scrapers to clean the floor. Back behind the cabin he found a rusty tin bucket, the sides mashed together, half-buried in the ground. Two holes were rusted in the bottom and the bail loose at one end.

Nathan pulled the sides apart, took a wad of dry grass and scoured the bucket clean; then he tore a piece from the rags and pulled it tight through the holes and tied on the bail where it was loosened. "It will hold water," he thought gratefully as he filled it at the spring, brought it back, and set it close to the fire where it would warm.

While the duck was cooking, he scraped the floor, taking the trash outside where he threw it back in the trees.

The smell of the fowl cooking filled the room and Nathan suddenly realized how hungry he was. He added a sprinkle of salt from his little hoard Ma had given him and sipped the broth. It was tasty enough for Pa to drink. Later, after the broth simmered, it would be thick and more nourishing. He dipped a few spoonfuls out into the tin cup and went to Pa. Kneeling beside the pallet, he lifted Pa's head and put a spoonful in his mouth. "Swallow, Pa," Nathan urged. Finally Pa swallowed.

"Good," Pa managed to whisper.

"Have more." Nathan gave him another spoonful and he swallowed again. After a few more spoonfuls he let his father lie back on the blanket.

"That's all for now," he told him as he pulled the blanket up under his father's chin. "After you rest a bit, I'll clean you up and you'll feel better. And Pa," Nathan leaned close and patted his father's shoulder, "*YOU ARE GOING TO GET WELL AND RIDE MAJOR BACK TO POOSEY. KEEP THINKING THAT.*"

Pa did not seem to hear. Nathan looked closely at him. If Grandpa were only here, or Dr. Maberry. They'd know what to do. What if Pa died, now he'd found him? He dared not face it. "I'll believe he will get well." He squared his shoulders. "And I'll work, too."

When the duck was tender Nathan fed his father more broth. Only a little at a time, but often. He looked at his father's hair and beard. The only thing to do was cut them off. He sharpened his knife on his boot and knelt beside the pallet.

"Pa, I'm going to trim your hair and beard. You'll feel better." Pa did not answer and Nathan, frightened, felt of his pulse. It was still there.

Most of Pa's hair came out in handfuls when Nathan started to cut it, so he shaved his father's head. Most of his beard came out, too. So Nathan cut and shaved and Pa lay without any sign that he felt it. He looked like an old withered skeleton with the dark curly hair and beard gone. Nathan stopped, afraid he had used up the last shred of his father's strength.

"Pa I'm through for now. You rest and we'll have more soup."

There was no answer. Nathan shook his father's shoulder. "Are you all right? Tell me, Pa?"

There was a faint nod and Nathan slumped, limp with relief. He went outside where he could not see his father and tried to think what to do. Should he go back to Lexington for Dr. Maberry? Or on to Carrollton where he might get help? But Dr. Maberry might be gone for a day or night and he knew his father was too far gone to be moved. What kind of a doctor would he make if he gave up this quickly? Grandpa always said, "While there's life, there's hope." And Pa was still alive, but barely so.

He went back inside to load his rifle, ending it up and pouring a measure of powder from the powder horn into the muzzle. Then he took a bullet, put one of Ma's grease squares around it and rammed it down the barrel with the ramrod. He laid it across his knee and poured a little powder in the priming pan, let the hammer down carefully and leaned the rifle in a corner against the wall.

He took Sam down to the lake to drink with Major following, then he staked out the mule behind the cabin. There were tracks where wild animals drank including the print of a bear.

Shadows were long across the little clearing when Nathan took the gun and went down to the lake. He walked to the edge to crouch behind some brush, watching the spot where the animals had made tracks. The sun set. It was quiet except for the quacking of the ducks feeding. Nathan waited.

Out of the forest came a trim doe with two half-grown fawns jumping and playing, the doe proud and alert. He could not bring himself to shoot.

"I'll wait," he decided. "Maybe a single one will come." The deer drank and went away. Nathan waited.

It was almost dark when two half-grown bucks came to the water. Nathan took aim and fired. One of them fell, the other bounded away into the forest.

Nathan shouldered the buck and hurried back. There was barely light enough to draw it and hang it on a tree near the cabin. Tomorrow he would skin it. He sliced the liver, put it on a stick and held it over the coals. When it was cooked, he ate hungrily. Pa had more soup which he seemed to swallow more easily.

Nathan brought in chunks of wood to keep the fire,

reloaded his rifle, and pulled and tugged on the door, but it would not close completely. Then he spread out his own blanket by the fire and lay down. He had hardly stretched out when there was a nickering and pawing at the door.

Pa made a sound and Nathan went to him. "Major," Pa whispered.

"I'll let him in," Nathan said and went to the door and pulled it wide open. Major came in, looked over toward Pa, and took his stand by the door where he had evidently stood for many nights.

Nathan stood beside Major for a moment and stroked his neck. "You're a fine horse, Major. Smart as any human. Smarter than some," he told the horse. Then he lay down again beside the fire.

—≫| CHAPTER 21 |≪—

I t seemed to Nathan he had hardly fallen asleep when pandemonium broke loose outside. Sam was snorting and plunging. Major whinnied and dashed outside. Nathan snatched his gun on his way to the door. In the darkness he could make out a dark form beside the deer carcass. It growled tearing at the meat with guttural sounds. A full-grown bear! Nathan dared not shoot. He could not see to aim. A wounded bear was a terrible thing! It might charge into the cabin and kill them both. His heart pounded in his throat.

He grabbed the unburned end of a blazing chunk of wood from the fireplace, stepped outside and flung it at the bear with all his strength. There was a horrible, chilling roar when the fire hit and the bear dropped down on all fours, the chunk of wood blazing beside him.

Nathan stood, rigid, breathless. For an awful instant he thought the bear was going to charge! Then it growled, and vanished in the darkness.

Nathan went to the deer, his knees weak. The front quarters had been mauled and partly eaten. Claw marks cut across the hind quarters, but there was enough good meat left to make a roast for him and stew for Pa.

Sam still charged in circles behind the cabin and Major circled in front, wild-eyed. Nathan came in squatting by Pa. "It was a bear after the deer meat," he said trying to keep his voice steady, "but it's gone now. I'm going to build a fire out front and roast what's left of the deer. The fire will protect us, too."

Pa nodded.

Nathan built the fire then skinned and cut away the torn part of the deer. He cut it in chunks sticking it on sticks around the fire. He cut up small chunks of meat and almost filled the little kettle. This would make fine soup for Pa, the more meat, the better it would be. He covered it with water and set it on the coals in the fireplace.

Behind the cabin Sam snorted and tramped. Nathan brought him around to the front. He dragged up part of a dead log and put it on the fire. It would burn until morning.

Dog-tired he lay down again. "Good night, Pa," he mumbled and pulled up the blanket.

"'Night," came faintly from the pallet.

When Nathan awoke, sunlight was touching the tops of the trees along the lake. Outside the flames flickered along the half-burned log. The roasting meat made Nathan's mouth water.

"You awake, Pa?" Nathan asked as he pulled on his boots. "Going to be a fine day!" He looked in the kettle, then went to the pallet. "You have good, fresh broth for breakfast. Thick and strong. It will give you strength." Pa had a whole cup of the liquid, then a drink of water.

"Good, so good," Pa said slowly as Nathan let him back on the blanket. For the first time a faint smile flickered across his face.

"Pa! You're better! Lot's better! You smiled!"

Pa smiled again.

After breakfast, Nathan went to Pa with the soap and a clean rag. Carefully he managed to get Pa's arms and legs out of his linsey shirt, undershirt and cotton drawers. His breeches were gone. Nathan's stomach twisted at Pa's terrible condition. If he hadn't been as strong as a mule he would never have survived. With a lather of lye soap he washed Pa, head and all, turning him on his side, heartsick at the sight of his father's back.

The pallet of old rags was filthy. Pa sure had to come off of that. Nathan covered his father and went outside to cut great armfuls of small leafy twigs. He carried them inside to make a pallet in the opposite corner. Then he spread his own blanket over the leaves and carried his father's naked body to the clean pallet.

Pa went limp and lifeless. "Hold on a little longer, Pa. I've clean clothes Ma sent from home. You'll feel better. I know you will. Hold on!" But Pa was so exhausted he could not even nod when Nathan finished putting on his clothes. He covered Pa with his other blanket, tucking it under his chin and over the shaven head. A terrible sinking in his own stomach. Pa had so little strength.

Nathan picked up the old pallet, piling Pa's clothes and blankets on top and dragged it outdoors. The clothes and blankets he carried to the lake where in a little shallow place he weighted them down with a rock to soak. While they soaked, he burned the pallet and scraped the floor where the pallet had been.

Pa slept for a long time after the bath. When he awoke Nathan gave him a full cup of broth and he slept again.

In the afternoon, Nathan took off his boots, rolled up his breeches, got in the lake to wash the blankets and clothes, scrubbing them between his hands until the lye soap was only a thin sliver, but the things were clean. Nathan wrung them out and spread them over the bushes near the cabin to dry. He would have to sleep close to the fire tonight, for the blankets would not be dry until tomorrow.

By night, Nathan could tell Pa was much better. "I had a good sleep on my clean bed," he told Nathan, "and I'm hungry."

"You are better, Pa! Lots better!"·

"Have to get better with such good doctoring."

Nathan flushed with the praise. "It won't be long until we can start home. Tomorrow I will walk along the lake and see if I can find some persimmons to help out with our meat. The more you eat, the sooner you'll get well and the sooner we can start home. If I had a fishhook, I'd catch us some fish."

"I had some hooks and lines . . . but they took them." Pa frowned and shook his head weakly. "They took my rifle . . . my boots . . . jacket . . . breeches . . . everything. They thought I was . . . dying." Pa was quiet for a long time and Nathan waited, worried that Pa was overdoing. "I was so sick with ague . . . that's why I stopped here in the . . . first place. Chills . . . and fever . . . seemed your Ma was here."

Exhausted he drifted off to sleep, but that evening he tried to tell more of his story. "The Indians . . . took my things . . . must have been a camp near. At first . . . one old squaw brought me . . . things to eat . . . bitter tea to drink. Then I got the smallpox. Must have caught it . . . from a sick man I helped . . . going down . . . The Indians went away . . . but Major came back. Sometimes it seemed . . . I was looking right into his face, but of course I wasn't." Pa stopped, tired out.

"I think you were," Nathan said. "There were hoof-prints right beside the pallet. Tomorrow you can tell me more and I've things to tell you when you get better."

In the morning after Pa was fed, Nathan went to look for persimmons. It was a late September day, high overhead a flock of wild geese winged their way southward and a soft blue haze veiled the distance across the lake. Indian summer, folks called it in Kentucky. Trees had started to turn and some were a brilliant yellow or a flaming red. Nathan thought of how Ma liked the fall. "Just my time of year," she always said. A sharp stab of homesickness swept over him, not for Kentucky, but for Ma and Betsy and Andy. Even Belle and Trinket.

Not far up the trail, Nathan found a persimmon tree, the pinkish-yellowish fruit hanging thick on the bare branches. Underneath the tree the fallen fruit lay juicy ripe. He stuck a soft one in his mouth, not a mite puckery and sweet as sugar. He spit out the seeds and took another and another. They were good! He lined his cap with dry leaves and filled it with the ripe fruit. Not far away a huge hickory tree had branches heavy with nuts. Nathan had never seen such large ones. He filled his pockets then started back.

Pa was awake and had turned on his side. He smiled at Nathan.

"Pa! You've turned over! Oh Pa, you're getting well fast! Look, I did find ripe persimmons." He held out his cap, picked out an extra big, soft one and put it in Pa's mouth. "Got hickory nuts, too," he said as he emptied his pockets and put the nuts by the fire to dry.

That night Pa ate a cup and a half of stew with small pieces of meat and another persimmon. "Keep that up," Nathan told his father, "and we'll soon be going home."

The good weather held and Pa got a little stronger each day. Nathan told him about the new cabin, about everything that happened on the trip, and then about having the patent sewed in his undershirt. Pa reached up to feel the envelope through Nathan's shirt. It was almost more than he could believe.

Finally, Pa could sit up awhile with the blanket over his

shoulders. Every day he ate more and at the end of three weeks, a half inch of dark, curly hair covered his head, a thick stubble of beard on his face. With Nathan's help, he managed to stand up, then his knees crumpled and he had to lie down again.

"I'll rub your legs and that will help to limber them," Nathan tried to console him.

"Too limber now," Pa said with a weak smile.

Nathan laughed. "Pa, it's good to have you joke again."

The next morning Pa took a step, and that afternoon Nathan urged him to try again. He took three. "When you can walk across the room by yourself, Pa, we're going to start home."

That evening while Nathan went to the spring to get water, he heard horses coming from the direction of Carrollton. He turned to run to the cabin for his gun, but it was too late. Scrunching down behind some bushes, he remembered all the things he had been warned about.

Two men on horseback came in sight. They stopped at the path to the cabin so near Nathan could hear what they said.

"There's a shack back in there. Let's stay the night," a deep voice said.

"Not there! I ain't about to stay there," a high squeaky voice answered. "It's haunted! Man and his horse died in there and their ghosts come out and chase ye."

"I ain't scairt," the deep voice said. He turned his horse toward the path back to the cabin and a high shrill whinny cut the air!

The high squeaky voice yelled with terror, whirled and

spurred his horse toward Lexington. The gruff one raised in his stirrups and fired a rifle shot toward the cabin as his horse plunged ahead.

Nathan stood up and watched them go, the men leaning low on the horses' necks. He picked up the bucket of water and ran toward the cabin.

Pa was leaning against the door jamb, looking toward the lake. "Nathan? What's happening? I heard a shot and horses running!"

"Men looking for a hideout! They knew about this place, but one thought it was haunted by a ghost and his horse. Then Major whinnied!" Suddenly Nathan stared. "Pa! You got to the door by yourself!"

"So scared it gave me strength," Pa said turning toward his pallet. Nathan started to help, but Pa motioned him aside. He almost fell on the pallet and pulled the blanket over him. He looked up at Nathan triumphantly. "Son, when can we start?"

"In the morning, Pa," Nathan said jubilantly. "There's a bank of clouds in the northwest and a feel of change in the weather. We better be getting out of here. Somebody else might come along and not be afraid of ghosts. It can't be far to Pete Johnson's and he'll take us in for as long as we need to stay."

—⇛ CHAPTER 22 ⇚—

A t daylight they had eaten and were ready to start. Gray clouds raced across the sky, a cold wind blew from the northwest. Spits of sleet stung Nathan's face. They were not getting out any too soon. He put the saddle and bridle on Major.

Pa had a folded blanket around his shoulders and Nathan's cap on his head, ear flaps down. Over the blanket was the oilcloth cape. Around Pa's feet Nathan wrapped the rags and tied them. The cup, plate and spoon were in the little kettle inside the mended bucket and the grubsack hung on the saddlehorn.

He put a blanket on the saddle, helped Pa up on a stump so he could get astride Major; then he wrapped the blanket around Pa's legs and tucked it in.

Nathan followed on Sam, sitting on a blanket with only a halter to guide the mule, his rifle on his shoulder. As they went around the fallen tree, Nathan looked back at the little cabin. That morning he had burned the lump of sulphur on the dirt floor, Grandma's remedy for killing contagious diseases. He had put out the fire and closed the door as far as it would shut. Already it looked lonely and forsaken.

Major knew he was going home. He struck out at a long, swinging walk, Sam close behind. They had been on the way over an hour when Nathan asked Pa if he wanted to stop and rest a spell.

Pa shook his head. "Soon be there," he said, his face drawn. So they went on. The trail kept going uphill. Nathan knew Carrollton was on a bluff so it could not be much farther.

Pa was slumping in the saddle. Nathan rode up beside him and reached out a hand. "Pa, I hear dogs barking. I see a roof. Pa?" Pa's face was gray, his eyes almost closed. An awful fear clutched Nathan. He slid from Sam to walk along beside Major, reaching up to steady Pa. "We're here, Pa! We're at Carrollton. Don't give up now." He shook his father's arm to keep him conscious. "I can see Pete Johnson's house right down the road."

He yelled for Pete, holding on to Pa, afraid he would fall from the saddle. Pete Johnson came from behind the cabin, a game sack over his shoulder, carrying his rifle. He stared at Pa, then looked at Nathan. "Why, it's Nathan Robison!"

"Pete, it's Pa! He's been awful sick and is clean tuckered out. Can we stay for the night?"

"Why ask? Let's get him inside the cabin."

They got Pa inside and put him in a chair in front of the fire. Nathan unfastened the blankets and began rubbing him.

"I'll warm up the coffee," Pete said as he stirred up the fire and set on the pot. "Something hot inside will start his blood to circulatin'. Below freezin' outside and that wind goes right through a feller."

He poured steaming chicory coffee into a cup holding it out to Pa, but Pa's hand shook so that Nathan had to hold it to his lips.

"While you give him another cup, I'll take care of the horse and mule. I remember you were real perticular about that mule," Pete chuckled. "I'll bring the saddle and bridle inside."

By the time Pa had had another cup of coffee and warmed by the fire he dozed off to sleep. Pete Johnson came back in. "Startin' to snow. I tied your mule and horse in the shed with the cow until the storm's over. Gave them hay. Looks like winter's here. Think you made it just in time."

"I didn't think it was so far," Nathan said. "Thought we'd make it in less than an hour, but we've been a lot longer than that."

"When did you leave Lexington? Where'd you find your father?"

"I went from here to the Land Office and found out Pa had been there, but that was all they knew. The patent had come back from Washington the day before tho' so I signed for it and have it with me." Nathan patted his shirt.

"Everyone warned me not to take the shortcut, but I'd been the long way and hadn't found Pa. There wasn't a thing to do but take the shortcut." Nathan told about finding Pa.

Pete Johnson's face paled and he leaned back in his chair. "You tell me your Pa's just gettin' over smallpox? How long since you first found him? How many days?" He stared at Nathan in horror. "Don't you know you could have smallpox and spread it everywhere?"

"But I've been vaccinated. I'm not going to take it. Besides it has been more than fourteen days since I found Pa."

"But his clothes? His blankets?"

"I shaved Pa's head and face and washed him with lye soap all over! I burned the pallet where he caught smallpox. I scraped the floor. I washed his clothes and the blankets. I burned sulphur in the cabin before we left. Just no way anybody could get it from us," Nathan said firmly.

Pete Johnson looked hard at Nathan thinking over all that he had said. Finally he seemed relieved. "You're right. It has been more than fourteen days. Been more than a month since you left here. You're telling the truth, but it's sure hard to believe. I never thought for one minute you'd ever find your Pa when you left here." He shook his head and stood up. "I'll warm up the mulligan I made yesterday, then your Pa can stretch out by the fire and sleep. You're welcome to stay until he feels good enough to travel."

Nathan smiled gratefully. "I told Pa if we could make Pete Johnson's, we'd be all right."

Pete's face reddened. "You'll never know how fightin' mad I felt for a minute, thinkin' you had smallpoxed me."

The storm lasted for two days before it cleared and the weather warmed up. The skim of ice and snow soon melted. Pete gave Pa a pair of his breeches and some socks and an old cap. Nathan bought a pair of moccasins for Pa at the trading post, which took nearly all of his money.

The morning of the third day Pa got up feeling real good, joking and visiting with Pete as he walked around the room.

"Pa, do you feel good enough to start home tomorrow?"

Pa straightened his thin shoulders. "I think I feel good enough to start this morning. Sun is warm and we might get halfway to Chillicothe."

"You're sure you feel good enough?" Pete asked. "You seem to feel pretty good mornings but by night you've lost your strength. Remember how done in you were when you got here? Welcome to stay longer."

Pa thanked him. "I remember and I won't ever forget you taking us in."

Within half an hour they were ready. Pete packed food in the bucket and fastened a cloth over the top tying it behind Pa's saddle; then he helped Pa mount. Nathan wrapped him in the blankets.

Nathan held out his hand to Pete. "We won't ever forget," he said. "Come and see us so we can pay the debt."

"No debt." Pete's voice was husky. "Proud to do it."

Heading for home, Major set the pace and Sam

followed close behind. The trail was a little muddy from the snow, but bee hunters' wagons had made tracks to follow.

They stopped about noon by a fallen tree where Pa could step off, and ate some of the victuals while Major and Sam rested. Pa stretched out on the tree trunk with a blanket over him. He looked so thin and frail, his cheeks and eyes sunken, that Nathan was afraid they had started home too soon. Maybe they should make camp right here by the fallen tree. But when he mentioned it Pa shook his head. "Thinking about being so close to home is good medicine. Let's go another hour or two and that ought to put us might near halfway to Chillicothe."

Nathan watched for a camping place. The middle of the afternoon he saw a huge hollow tree standing close to the trail where someone had camped before. Dead campfire ashes were in front of the opening to the tree. There was room for one person to sleep inside where it would be dry and warm.

Pa was ready to stop for the night. Nathan spread a blanket in the tree and helped his father inside. "Not as pert as I thought I was," Pa sighed as he lay down on the blanket. Nathan covered him with another.

Nathan built a fire on the ashes of the old one and heated a slice of the venison Pete had given them. Pa ate and went to sleep.

It would be a long, cold night. Nathan wished it was over. He hunted for firewood and dragged up part of a dead log. He would need to keep the fire going all night.

Days were short and dark came early in the timber. He took off the saddle and tied Major and Sam near the hollow tree then rubbed them both. "I know you're hungry and thirsty, but I can't risk hobbling you," he told them.

Nathan ate a bite, wrapped a blanket around himself and sat down near the opening of the tree. He leaned against the rough bark, the rifle beside him and the darkness settled down.

Far away came the howl of a wolf and not so far away another answered. Nathan's skin crawled. He could hear Major and Sam move uneasily. He leaned over to stir the fire into a blaze then pulled the blanket close, his hand on the rifle. Finally the wolf cries faded away and Nathan went to sleep.

It was getting daylight when a sudden, wild banging and growling ripped the stillness, yanking Nathan wide awake. Across from the dying fire a dark form plunged and rolled on the ground clawing and growling! Nathan grabbed the loaded rifle and cocked it. A bear had his head caught in the tin bucket! He aimed at the bucket, but the frantic animal lurched and writhed so he dared not shoot. Then with a maddened roar, the bear tore the bucket loose and lunged straight at Nathan!

Nathan fired and jumped to his feet. The bear came on! He grabbed the rifle by the barrel and brought the butt down on the bear's head just as it fell against the tree, dead from the shot!

"Whew!" Pa said as he came out of the tree. "That was a close call." He looked at Nathan leaning white-faced against the tree. "I guess there's more than one way to kill a bear, but I never heard of clubbing one to death!"

Nathan tried to answer, but his teeth chattered so he could not speak. He slumped down beside the bear letting out a long, shuddering breath. "It's too early in the morning . . . to be killing bears," he said weakly.

"You didn't have much choice," Pa said as he leaned over the bear. "It's a half grown one. Guess he smelled the honey Pete gave us. Must have had his mind on going to sleep for the winter, or he wouldn't have come this close. Give me a hand and we'll drag him over here to skin him so that we can have fresh meat for breakfast."

By the time they had skinned the bear and had breakfast the sunlight was slanting through the trees. "While you pack up, Nathan, I'll rest a mite. Been a long time since I helped skin a bear. Tuckered me out."

Pa looked ready to drop. In the excitement Nathan forgot how weak Pa was, how little strength he had. And they weren't home yet. Pa seemed to forget, too.

He had cooked extra meat to put in the bucket and with the grub bag tied it on the saddlehorn. The two hind quarters of the bear he put inside the skin and wrapped it with the picket rope. Major snorted and side-stepped when Nathan heaved it up behind the saddle.

When the sun was straight overhead Nathan thought they should be nearing the river. Pa had not said a word for a long time and was bent over in the saddle. Nathan knew he should rest. If something happened to Pa now, he would never forgive himself. When they came to a grassy spot, he helped Pa down and spread out a blanket. Pa dropped off to sleep as soon as he finished eating.

Nathan watched the sky for sunshine, but it was gone and clouds scudded overhead. A chilly wind blew up from the north. He woke Pa. "We better be getting on. A storm is blowing up and we might have to ford the river if the ferry isn't running."

He helped Pa into the saddle and they started up the trail.

—⇥| CHAPTER 23 |⇤—

It was beginning to rain when they came to the river at Jimtown. There was no sign of a ferry, but across the river Nathan could see a dugout tied up at the bank. He remembered how deep and strong the current had been when he crossed before. Now the water seemed even higher, muddy with silt and swirling in dark eddies.

Nathan looked at Pa humped over in the saddle. He knew his father could never ford the river. "I'll yell for the man to come and ferry us across in the dugout," Nathan said and Pa nodded.

Nathan cupped his hands around his mouth and shouted with all his strength. Then he waited, but no one came. He shouted again and again, but the only answer was the beat of the rain. In an hour it would be dark. They had not passed a cabin for miles, if they could only get across the river, the storekeeper at Jimtown would surely put them up for the night. Once more Nathan shouted, but there was no answer. He knew then what he had to do.

"Pa, I'll leave you and the rifle and bear meat here and swim the horses over and come back for you in the dugout."

Pa shook his head. "It looks bad, Nathan, and near dark. Shouldn't we wait until morning?"

"Pa, you can't stand to stay out all night in this weather. It's going to freeze and there's no let-up in the rain. We've got to get across sometime, so let's try it now."

Pa gave a deep sigh and his dark eyes were troubled when he looked at Nathan. "You're the one that has to do it. I'll be no help, but Son, be mighty careful. Don't try to lead Sam. Tie up his halter rope and he'll follow Major."

"I'll be back as soon as I can make it," Nathan promised as he climbed on Major. He walked the horse across the sandbar, dreading the moment they would be in the water, fearing the strong current. Major dreaded it too, for he stopped at the edge of the river and Nathan had to make him step into the water. Sam followed behind them. Nathan headed the horse upstream, knowing he would drift down with the current.

They were almost halfway across before they were in deep water and Major started swimming. Nathan stood up in the stirrups and the current swirled around his waist and pulled at his legs like a living thing. Major was almost to the bank when he began thrashing around and struggling.

"Major! Major! Get out of here! Get!"

With an awful effort the horse reached the bank, but it was so steep he could not find a foothold. Nathan grabbed a low-hanging tree branch and holding the rein, pulled himself out on the bank.

Slipping and sliding in the mud, he edged his way along the river bank holding onto branches, pulling on the bridle reins, trying to keep Major's head above water. Sam had found a place and had climbed out.

"Get! Get!" Nathan yelled as he pulled on the reins. Snorting and blowing, Major struggled up on the bank and stood trembling, his head hanging, water running from his nostrils. Shocked, Nathan saw that a vine was so tangled around Major's hind feet that he could hardly move them.

"Oh, Major," Nathan choked on the words. "You almost drowned." He pulled the vine from Major's legs. One of them was cut and bleeding.

Trying to hurry, Nathan tied Major and Sam then went back to the dugout. It was tied to a tree and there was a paddle in the bottom of the boat, but the rope was wet and the knot so hard that Nathan's fingers, cold and stiff, could hardly loosen the knot. Finally he climbed into the boat.

Out on the river, the force of the wind struck him and the rain beat in his face. The whole world seemed made of water. Dimly through the coming darkness, he could see the sandbar. He headed for it. Paddling first on one side and then the other, Nathan tried to guide the boat. At last he touched the sandbar.

"Pa, I'm back," he called. "We'll have to hurry. It's a

bad landing on the other side. Never could find our way in the dark." He helped Pa to the boat, then went back for the rifle, bear meat, and other things. Every muscle ached as he staggered under the load of the meat. Numbly, he wondered how he could ever carry it up the steep bank on the other side.

It was almost dark when they got across. Nathan tied up the dugout, then carefully helped Pa out of the boat. Pushing and pulling, he got him up the bank and, finally, onto Major. He felt utterly exhausted.

He leaned against the horse for a few minutes, and Pa spoke to him. "Nathan? Are you all right?"

"Yes . . . I just had to catch my breath . . . I'll get the blankets . . ." He started down to the boat, his cold, wet clothes clinging to him, water squashing in his boots. He wondered dimly if he would ever be dry and warm again.

At the boat, he gathered up the blankets, grubsack and bucket carrying them to the top where Pa was waiting.

"Oh, the bear meat . . .," he mumbled and started back. At the boat, he waited a moment before stepping in to pick up the meat. Taking a long breath, he leaned over and lifted it, clutching his fingers in the hair, hugging it to him. Somehow, he must find the strength to get it up the bank. But as he stepped out, the boat rocked beneath him and he stumbled and slipped, crying out as the meat fell with a splash and disappeared in the deep water!

Nathan stood for a moment, staring at the place where the meat had vanished. Then he turned and, empty handed, climbed the steep bank, too tired to care.

"It fell in the water," Nathan said dully when he got back to Pa.

Pa didn't answer.

Rather than try to mount, he led Sam to the storekeeper's house, his father following on Major. He knocked and shouted, the dogs barked, but no one answered. For a moment, Nathan felt he could go no farther, but Pa had to have shelter . . . and he himself wanted a fire . . . a nice, warm fire.

"There is a house up the trail about a mile," he told Pa. "We'll try to make it. . . . If they aren't home, maybe we can go on to Chillicothe . . . ," his voice trailed off into the darkness. He put one of the blankets around him, found a stump, and struggled onto Sam's back. But the wind seemed to blow right through the blanket, and his legs felt paralyzed.

Cold, weary, and limping a little, Major plodded ahead with Sam following. An eternity later, a spot of light shone through the darkness.

Nathan reached out and turned Major into the clearing. "Anybody home?" he called out hoarsely.

The door opened and a tall man stood in the light. "Who's there?" he asked.

"Nathan Robison and his father," Nathan replied through chattering teeth. "Pa's been sick. Could you take us in for the night?"

"Git off and come in. We'll make room," the man said.

Nathan slid stiffly from Sam's back and led Major close to the door. Pa almost fell as Nathan reached up to help him. The man grabbed his arm guiding him into the cabin.

"So cold," Pa mumbled as they set him down in a chair by the fire. Nathan tried to take off the cape of blankets, but his hands shook so he almost dropped them. Two little girls watched, round-eyed.

"Why, you're shaking! You're wet!" the woman exclaimed. "No wonder you're cold! Is it raining that hard?"

"No, I had to ford the river horseback." Nathan tried to still his chattering teeth. "Then I took a boat back and got Pa."

The man went to the wall where clothes were hanging on a peg. He came back to Nathan. "Our name's Pinkerton and here's a pair of my breeches. Rosie and the girls will turn their backs. You shuck off your wet ones and hang them by the fire. Take your death of cold settin' around in them wet ones. I'll get your Pa settled."

Nathan thought he had never felt anything so warm as the dry breeches. He pulled off his boots and socks, then his breeches and drawers, and slipped into the dry ones. The tails of his linsey shirt and undershirt were wet, but the patent seemed only damp up under his arm. He let his shirttails hang outside; they would soon dry. The woman spread his clothes before the fire and Nathan put his boots and socks on the hearth.

"I'll bring your saddle in the house then tie your animals in the shed with a bit of hay. Where you folks comin' from?"

"We left Carrollton yesterday and we're on our way to Poosey, up beyond Navestown," Nathan told him.

"Say! You ain't the boy that the storekeeper told about

that left here weeks ago to find his pa, be ye? He came from that place Poosey."

"Yes, I'm the one," Nathan said tiredly.

"And you found him! By golly! That's a miracle!"

Mrs. Pinkerton brought stew with cornbread and some hot chicory coffee to them. Pa tried to tell them about Nathan shooting the bear, but he couldn't finish so Nathan had to tell them he had lost the bear meat and hide in the river.

"What a shame!" the man exclaimed. "All that good meat gone to waste!"

Nathan shook his head. It seemed unimportant now. . .

Mrs. Pinkerton brought a thick comforter to spread before the fire. Pa lay down on it and she covered him with a blanket. He was snoring in a few minutes.

Soon the family went to bed and Nathan lay down by Pa. Every bone ached. He was still cold. He felt as if he could lie there before the fire forever. Outside, the wind howled, rain beat against the roof. He hoped Sam and Major were dry now in the shed. . . . Anyway, they were on the Poosey side of the river, he thought as he drifted off to sleep.

It was afternoon the next day when Nathan saddled Major to get ready to leave. Major and Sam were cold and Nathan knew they were hungry. The sky was overcast with a sharp wind blowing when they started out. They did not stop at Chillicothe.

As they came down the long, steep hill that led to Grand River and the ferry, Nathan looked to the Northwest where Indian Hill stood blue against the sky. That was only a little way from Navestown, Poosey and home!

At the ferry, Nathan rang the bell. A woman bundled in a man's jacket came from the cabin. "My man's gone huntin' and won't be back till sundown, but if you ain't afeared, I can take you over as good as he can."

"We're not afraid," Nathan said."Just so we get on the other side."

They were soon across. Nathan paid their fare and thanked her. It was his last coin, but it was the last river they had to cross.

At sundown they got to Navestown. Dick let out a yell when he saw them, "Ma! Pa! Everybody! It's Nathan and his Pa! They ain't dead! They're alive!"

Nathan pulled Major and Sam to a halt. "It's us, sure enough, but Pa's done in. He's been awful sick."

"Get off and stay the night," Jesse urged.

But Pa said, "No," his voice weak.

"We'll try to make it home," Nathan said.

"When you get well, we'll have a regular blowout! Fiddlin' and everything!" Jesse called out as they started on.

It was dark overhead, but a thin skift of snow made it light underfoot. Sam and Major plodded along, Pa bent lower and lower over the saddlehorn. Nathan was numb with cold and his mind blurred with tiredness.

When they came to the shed, Belle whinnied and Major stopped, but Nathan took his bridle rein and led him on to the house.

Shep came to meet them running, barking, in frantic circles. They stopped finally in front of the cabin.

"Ma? Ma? It's Nathan and Pa! We're here! We're here!" The door opened and Ma stood there, the firelight behind her, peering out into the dark.

"Nathan? Peter?" Her voice trembled.

"Here we are, Ma! Right Here! Pa and Major and Sam and me!" Nathan choked and couldn't say more as Ma came running toward him. He slid to the ground and she flung her arms around him laughing and crying. Betsy ran out and grabbed and kissed him. Together, they got Pa down from Major's back, up the step, into the house to a chair by the fire.

While Ma and Betsy were unwrapping Pa, Nathan went outside to unsaddle Major and take off Sam's halter. Belle stood nickering softly, Trinket beside her. The foal smelled of Nathan, then nuzzled his sleeve. Nathan slipped his arm around the foal's neck, but Belle pushed her nose between them. "I'm glad you didn't have to make the trip," he told her. "We had a hard, hard time."

Andy had waked up and was standing, looking at Pa. He ran to Nathan and took his hand. "Who's that man?" He pointed at Pa.

"That's our Pa. Don't you remember him?"

Andy shook his head and held onto Nathan.

While Ma was washing Pa's face and hands Betsy took off Pa's moccasins and Pete Johnson's socks.

"Nathan, help me get your Pa into clean drawers and undershirt while Betsy heats some stew. Then we'll put him to bed."

When they took off Pa's shirt Ma saw his pock-marked body, she put her arms around him and burst into tears.

Pa lifted his hand and slowly stroked Ma's hair. "Marthy, don't take on so," he said slowly. "I'm home again . . . our boy brought me home." He whispered the words like a prayer.

Nathan choked up. If Pa never said another word, that was thanks enough. After they put Pa to bed, Ma and Betsy kissed him, but Andy held back shaking his head.

Nathan sat down at the table with victuals before him, Ma and Betsy urging him to eat. He couldn't believe he was really home.

He was puzzled as he looked around the room. "Where did you get this table and the benches and the chair by the fire? And the blackboard? And the cut wood by the fireplace?"

Ma smiled. "You remember Jesse Nave was sure your Pa would never come back, that he was dead?" she reminded him. "Well, when you didn't come back after two weeks, he was sure you were lost or dead, too." Ma's eyes filled with tears again. "He came out and wanted me to move into the settlement to teach school in the Lamson house. The families were willing to give victuals and cut firewood for pay."

She looked deep into Nathan's eyes. "But I knew in my heart that you would find your Pa and bring him home. I just knew it, Nathan!" She reached across the table and laid her hand on Nathan's. "I prayed every day."

"I prayed, too," Betsy whispered.

"I told them I didn't want to leave my home. I wanted

to be here when you came back, but that if they'd send the children here, I'd be thankful to teach them. So the fathers made the benches and the chairs. Jesse Nave made and painted the blackboard extra. It's such a help."

"School started last week," Betsy added. "We have to use the books we brought from Kentucky and what Ma has in her head. Only three or four have any books, but Mr. Nave says he will get books to keep for trade in his store. Some have slates and some brought Bibles to read from. Nathan, some older than you can't read or write, but they want to learn. I helped Ma with the beginners."

"How many come?" Nathan asked.

"Ten came the first day, all from Navestown, but word got around. Today there were seventeen, three from up north beyond Panther Cave," Ma said.

"Seventeen? In this room?"

"There'll be more," Betsy said. "They are to come every day but Sunday as long as the weather isn't too bad."

"Will they come tomorrow?"

"No, tomorrow's Sunday."

An awful thought struck Nathan. Pa came to Missouri to get away from people. Now with a houseful, would he want to move again? Nathan pushed the thought away. He was too tired to think about it tonight.

"And we named it Poosey School and . . ."

Nathan tried to listen, but Betsy's voice faded away.

"Nathan! Nathan! Wake up! You're going to sleep sitting straight up. You're tired out!" Ma shook him.

"I'll just sleep by the fire," Nathan mumbled. "I can't climb the ladder tonight."

—⇒| CHAPTER 24 |⇐—

Nathan awoke to the sound of Ma humming soft little tunes and stirring something in a bowl for breakfast. Betsy was setting the table and Andy still sleeping.

He lay there for a few moments, groggy with sleep, the homey, comforting sounds all around him like a soft, warm cloak.

"What you cooking for breakfast, Marthy? Smells larrupin'," Pa said as he sat up on the side of the bed and put on his moccasins.

Ma laughed. "Corncakes and hominy, and I'm warming up some roasted prairie chicken."

"Prairie chicken? Where'd you get that?" Pa asked as he moved slowly toward the table.

"One of the children brought it. Oh, Peter, we've so much to tell you. I'm teaching school and the parents pay me with provisions and cut the wood."

Pa stopped, bewildered. "Teaching? Where?"

"Right here, in this room. They come from Navestown and up beyond Panther Cave and all around."

Pa sat down. "Here? In this room? How many?"

"Seventeen yesterday," Betsy answered, "but there'll be more. They are to come every day but Sunday until the weather gets bad. It's fun, Pa, and one day Ma made soup for everybody."

Ma put corncakes on their plates. Pa ate and listened while Betsy and Ma told everything that had happened.

Nathan waited, uneasy. What would Pa think about children filling up his home every day when he'd come clear from Kentucky to keep from being crowded?

Pa took a last bite then leaned back in his chair. He looked at Ma, a wry little smile on his face. "I'm right proud of you, Marthy, teaching school here in our little holler. Might even start up a singing class to help out. Anyhow, if the younguns get too thick, I can go outdoors," he joked.

Then Pa grew serious, his dark eyes thoughtful. "When I was so sick, my mind was so addled that it seemed Major and I were the only living things in the world. When I could think, I prayed for someone to come. I knew I was dying. Then Nathan came. I'll never again say I want to get clean away from people. Just forty acres with elbow room is all I ask."

A quiet peace flowed over Nathan. Maybe Dick was right. Pa would never want to move again.

"How did you ever find Pa?" Ma asked.

"Major came and led me to him," Nathan said simply.

After that, Nathan and Pa both talked. When they had

finally told it all, Nathan remembered; he took off his shirt, then his undershirt. "Been sewed there so long I almost forgot about it being there. Hope it didn't get too damp in the river."

He carefully took out the stitches Annie had put in. Pa's hands trembled as they took out the patent from the envelope and unfolded the thick parchment.

"The United States of America, to whom these presents shall come, Greetings," Pa read. "Whereas Peter Robison, entered into this tenth day of August, eighteen hundred and thirty-seven, A.D." He read the whole patent aloud, his voice proud when he came to the signature, Andrew Jackson, President of the United States.

"That means the land is ours, doesn't it?" Betsy asked, her eyes shining.

"Yes, but there's more than just the land," Ma said softly. "There's the creek and the spring, the cliff and the valley, the huge trees . . . and such good neighbors."

"And don't forget the antelope and deer, the 'coons and possums and all the other animals," Nathan went on.

"And the rattlesnakes!" Betsy shivered.

"And the house. It's a kind of miracle," Pa said. "When I left, it wasn't here. When I got back, it was." He gave a little sigh.

Ma spoke up. "Peter, you must lie down and rest."

"Marthy, I've something more to say." Pa stopped and seemed to be thinking. Firelight flickered on the walls and the clock chimed in the stillness. Nathan felt a sudden warming.

"Nathan, I know you wanted to stay in Kentucky with

your Grandpa and learn to be a doctor," Pa began slowly, head down. "Riled your feelings, having to come to Missouri, and I knew it. But a boy owes it to his Pa to help with the living until he's of age and a man. I had to make you come. It's hard work settling a new land.

"And I didn't hold with your Grandpa giving you big ideas, saying you had a natural bent for doctoring." Pa stopped, staring into the fire, and Nathan waited, his heart pounding. What was Pa driving at?

Then Pa looked straight at Nathan. "After you found me and cared for me, I knew your Grandpa was right. I made up my mind if I ever got home again and able to work, your debt was paid. You risked your life to find me. If you had not . . . I'd be dead today. Son, if you want to go back to Kentucky or study with the doctor in Lexington, I'll say nary a word against it. You're the same as a man grown."

Nathan tried to speak, but his throat was stiff and dry. "Pa . . . Pa . . . I sure . . . am obliged," He stumbled over the words. "I'll have to think . . . about when and where." He swallowed hard and his eyes misted. "But Pa, I won't go until you get back to feeling yourself again. I promise you that."

Pa nodded and got up, not very steady on his feet.

Nathan took his arm and helped him across the room. "Talking is hard work, when you got such big things to say," Pa said weakly, as he lay down on the bed.

Nathan got his jacket and went outside, his heart too full for words. Shep jumped up licking his hand then ran along beside him. The storm was over; sunshine filled the little valley, and the skift of snow was almost gone. He walked to the shed and Molly was there chewing her cud. Ma had turned her dry but she would soon have her calf. He would help Pa build on to the shed to make it a barn with a hayloft and door for protection from wild animals and bad weather. Surely there would come a day when he could go with Dick and Walkfast to explore Panther Cave.

Belle and Trinket were browsing near the creek, but the horses and mules had gone up the valley where the bluestem grew. He whistled and Trinket came to him. He petted her then looked carefully at the bark around her legs. Some of it was gone, but Trinket seemed not to need it. Nathan used his knife to cut the hickory strips that held it on then removed the last splints of bark. Underneath, Trinket's legs were straight, strong, and when Nathan finished, she kicked up her heels, free and happy as a boy when he shucks his long underwear in the spring.

Nathan stood watching the colt, the warm sun against his back, the last bit of resentment and loneliness slipping away. He looked back at the house he had helped to build, then to the high cliff, shining against the sky. Tracks of Sam and Major still marked the trail that led to Navestown and on beyond. Nathan knew he would travel it again when he went away, perhaps to study with Dr. Maberry and Annie, and later to Transylvania College at Lexington, Kentucky.

A sudden, wild idea almost took his breath away. He might even go on to Edinburgh or Paris to get his doctor's degree. He felt grown up and strong. Nothing was too much when you set your mind to it. He thought of the last few months, then of the years ahead. He knew finally, in his heart, that it was those he loved that made it home and not a certain thing or place.

He turned back toward the cabin whistling a little tune, at peace with himself. If he hurried there might be time to read a whole chapter in the doctor book.

ABOUT THE AUTHOR

My mother, Olive Cook, was born in 1892 on a farm not far from Poosey, and it was her home until she was eighteen. The farm, near the small town of Avalon, was about fifteen miles southeast of Chillicothe as the crow flies; Poosey, the center of it if there is such a thing as a center, is about the same distance from Chillicothe in the opposite direction (Northwest).

When she was eight her mother died and she turned to her grandmother for a close nurturing bond. It was probably from her grandmother that she heard so many of the expressions and words that were commonplace in Missouri in the early 1800's. Words no longer in daily use for us, but words that fall easily and appropriately into her story set in Missouri in the 1830's.

My mother knew the hard work of the frontier life she described in her book because many of her Mother's tasks fell to her on the farm. It was she, now, who cooked the huge meals for the workers during threshing season. One of the stories I remember Mom telling me was about a time shortly after her Mother's death when she baked a cake for an annual Easter church picnic, a time at which all the ladies of the church "strutted their stuff" with their fancy food. Although she remembered the cake being a dripping, gooey mess of thick layers of icing, her eyes twinkled when she recalled her father's pride announcing, "My daughter baked the white layer-cake."

Another childhood story she would tell me was about duck hunting. Ducks often landed on the pond near their house and one day when her father was gone, she decided to try to shoot one with his shotgun. Her arm wasn't long enough to reach the trigger when the gun was held normally, so she laid the gun down on the bank then stretched out on the ground beside it herself. She got it aimed and fired. She was very surprised and later sore from the results of a runaway, unrestrained gun.

Mother loved horses and rode a great deal as a girl. Even later when she went to horse shows a special gleam came into her eyes. One of her favorite horses on the farm broke her leg and the common wisdom of the neighboring farmers was that nothing could be done but to "put it out of its misery". Her father, however, did not listen to them and instead rigged a strong sling to suspend the horse from the rafters of the barn taking the weight off her leg. They gathered cobwebs, then, and wrapped them around the wound to stop the bleeding. Her horse's leg did heal.

Except for a six-month period, Mother lived in Chillicothe from the time she was eighteen until she was fifty years old. Because she lived so close to Poosey and also because she loved the outdoors with a natural curiosity about life, it is not surprising she would write a story with a setting in the strange, rather wild, undefined area of Poosey. The almost mythical descriptions of Poosey with its slippery boundaries were still abundant while my mother was writing her story in the 1960's and 70's. Now, however, the State of Missouri has declared Poosey a State

Forest and its boundaries are finally established—although I would not be a bit surprised if there is some disagreement among the local residents about the correctness of these boundaries.

The frontier and self sufficient life style were a central part in many of my mother's previous stories and books as well as in her own life. It is, therefore, appropriate that she picked the early frontier days of Missouri for her last tale. In addition to the childhood contact with her grandmother and her grandmother's wisdom, I remember her doing research on many of the small details for the book; research which included trips into Poosey to talk with the old timers there.

Joe Armstrong, a close and longtime friend of mine, was also a very close friend and admirer of my mother. They were kindred spirits in their feelings about the basics of life, keeping things simple and the virtues of being in touch with the land. She followed with great interest his giving up much of his professional life to establish a homestead near Healdsburg, California.

Joe has recently become a partner in Misty Hill Press, the publisher of this book. It seems a strange quirk of fate that Joe would be involved in the publication of her book. Such a strange coincidental ending would have seemed the most remote possibility up until quite recently. Mother would have been very surprised and pleased to have known that Joe would be involved in its publication. Too bad she is not around to enjoy the publication of *TRAILS TO POOSEY*, but I can assure you that her spirit lives on in the pages of the book—and maybe in some favorite spot in Poosey too!!

George Cook
March 12, 1986